MURDER AND CHIANTI

A BLAKE SISTERS TRAVEL MYSTERY—BOOK 6

CARTER FIELDING

Published by Carter Fielding Press
5237 River Road, #304
Bethesda, MD 20216

Editing, design, and production by Bublish, Inc.
ISBN (Paperback): 978-1-64704-877-8
ISBN (eBook):   978-1-64704-878-5

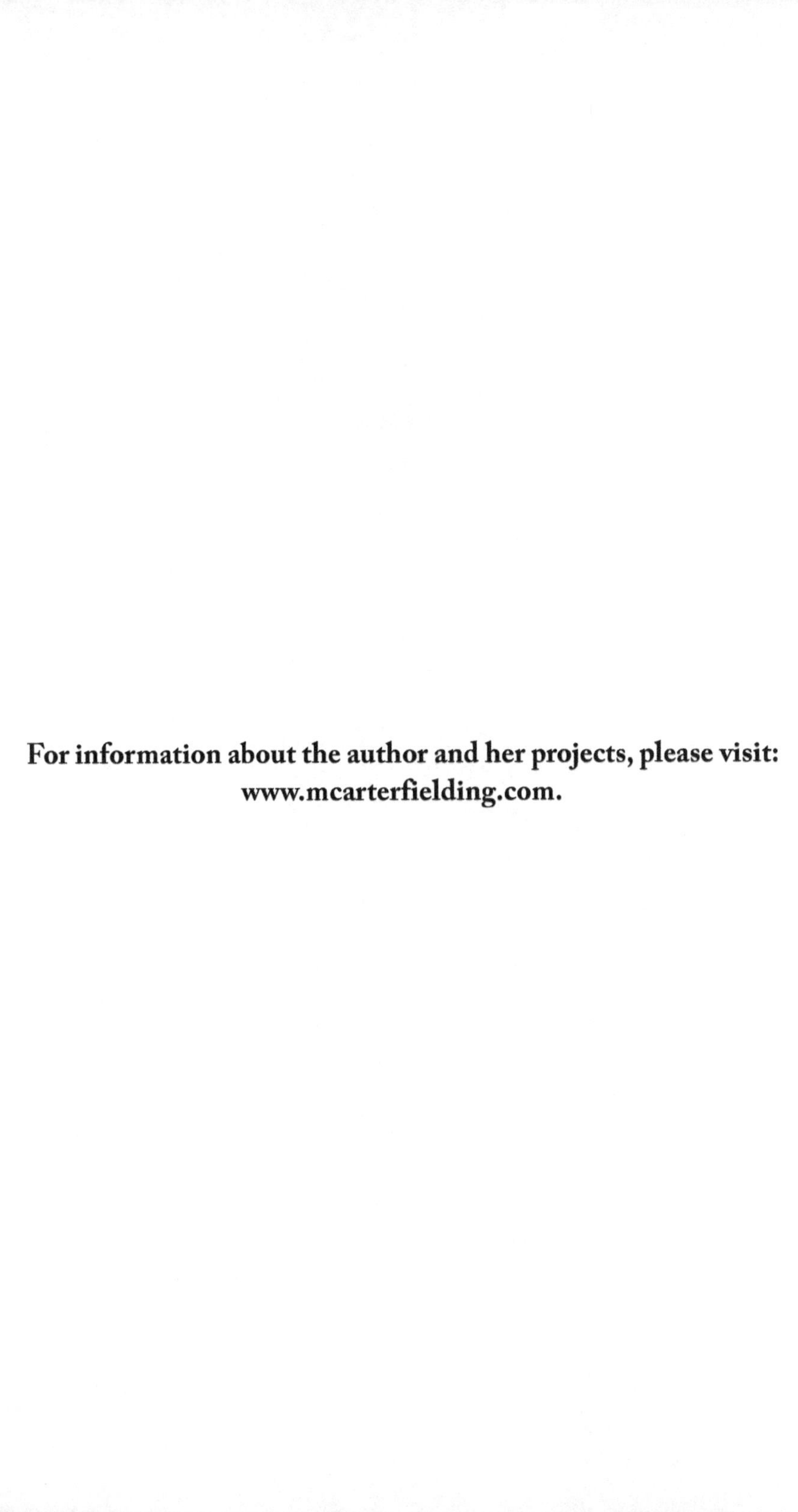

For information about the author and her projects, please visit:
www.mcarterfielding.com.

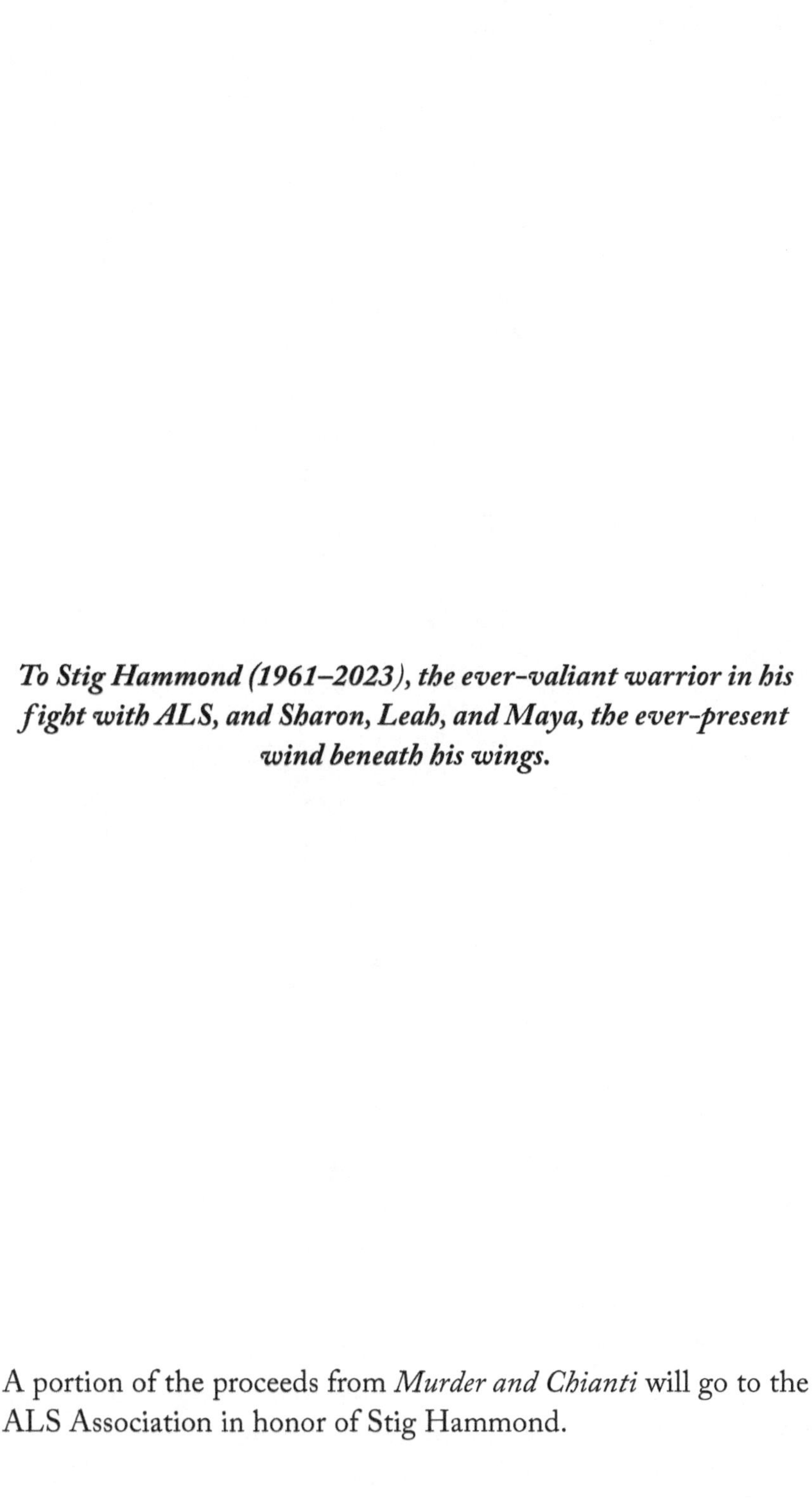

To Stig Hammond (1961–2023), the ever-valiant warrior in his fight with ALS, and Sharon, Leah, and Maya, the ever-present wind beneath his wings.

A portion of the proceeds from *Murder and Chianti* will go to the ALS Association in honor of Stig Hammond.

Works in the Blake Sisters Travel Mystery Series

Books
Murder in the Medina—Book 1
Murder in the Tea Leaves—Book 2
Murder with a Twist—Book 3
Murder in the Marshes—Book 4
Murder at the Summit—Book 5

Novellas
Murder in Montauk—Prequel
Murder on the Stairway to Heaven

Short Stories/Bonus Chapters
"Fes"
"London Bridges"
"Murder in Zanzibar"

Other Short Stories
"Past Is Past," *Creatures, Crimes & Creativity 2023 Anthology*

1

FINLEY BLAKE AND HER LIFE partner, Max Davies, were debating whether to stay in or go out for a late lunch one lazy Sunday in May when her phone buzzed. As she turned the page of the *New York Times* to continue reading an article that had caught her eye, she considered letting it ring. Whoever it was could call later or leave a text message.

But what if it's Mama? Or Whitt? What if something's happened?

The scenarios raced through her mind as the phone continued to ring. With Whitt and David in Tbilisi for the next several months and Mama and Daddy back in Chevy Chase, she was always unsettled by the distances between her in London and the rest of the family scattered all over the world. Given the long hours it would take to reach them in case of an emergency, would she get there in time?

She startled Max by jumping up from the kitchen table mid-sentence and grabbing her phone from the large marble island that was the heart of Max's mews house, now their home when they weren't traveling.

"Fin, what's wrong?" Max asked as she flipped over the phone and stared at the screen, temporarily frozen in place.

Her eyes remained fixed on her phone for several seconds before she heard her voice say his name. "Grant. It's Grant."

Grant, her ex-husband. The one who lived in Greenwich, Connecticut, with his darling petite, blonde, Junior League wife and their perfect two-children-and-a-dog family. Finley hadn't seen her ex in almost a decade, since returning from Morocco the first time. Then, she had been just on the other side of healing from a breakup with Max and had gone with Mooney Allen, her best friend and protector, to a gallery opening in Soho. The exchange with Grant and his wife there had been brief and cordial.

Max leaned back in his seat at the table. "What does he want?" His voice was neutral, betraying little beyond genuine curiosity.

"I don't know. Let's find out." Finley bit the inside of her lip and pressed the answer button. "Hello?"

There was a pause and then a rush of words, as if the connection had been broken before being quickly mended.

"Finley? Finley? This is Grant! Thank goodness, it worked." Grant's voice was excited, almost frantic. The patchy reception didn't help.

"Grant, what a surprise! How are you and—" Finley started before Grant cut in.

"Finley, I don't have much time. I'm in Spoleto. In jail. They say I killed Blaine. My wife. I didn't. They say I pushed her off the train. I swear I didn't. I didn't know where else to turn. I can't call my lawyer in the States. It would ruin me! Finley, for God's sake, help me!"

Finley's brow creased. "Grant, I'm not sure how I can. I'm not a practicing attorney, and even if I were, I can't practice in Italy. Why didn't you call a lawyer there?"

"I don't need a lawyer. I need a friend who can get to me quickly, help me think clearly." Grant's voice cracked. "I'm scared. I don't know what to do. Please help me!"

Finley could hear a staccato of words in Italian in the background. She covered the mike with her hand as she quickly turned to Max. "How's your Italian?"

"Passable," Max replied. "What's going on?"

Finley moved swiftly to the kitchen table and turned on the phone's speaker. The Italian directives continued in the background.

"Do you understand what they are saying?" Finley turned to Max and pushed the phone closer to him.

"It's hard to hear clearly, but I think they are telling him he has to end the call," Max whispered.

Grant returned to the phone, more frantic than before. "They say I have to go back to the cell. Finley, please help me!"

"Grant, calm down. Where exactly are you? You mentioned Spoleto."

Before she could get any more information, a man came on the line and began speaking roughly and rapidly in Italian. Max picked up the phone and moved it toward his mouth. Finley could understand very little of what was said for the next several minutes, but whatever Max said had changed the spout of directives into a seemingly cordial conversation. In time, Max grabbed a pen that was lying about and scribbled a name and address on the margin of the newspaper section he had been reading.

"*Grazie. Grazie mille per il suo aiuto*" was all she heard Max say before the screen went black.

"So, what's the deal?" Finley poured more coffee into Max's cup and then topped off hers. "Is he really in a Spoleto jail?"

Max nodded with a scowl on his face. "Charged with murdering his wife."

"That can't be right. Grant may be a lot of things, but he's not a killer."

"When did you last see him?"

"When I came back from Morocco the first time."

"That was ten years ago. A lot can change in that time."

Finley pondered what Max had said. A lot *had* changed in that time. She had returned to Morocco, run into Max, and ended up entering into a committed, permanent relationship with him, a lifelong partnership without marriage—an institution he abhorred for a range of reasons Finley understood and accepted. She suspected that Grant and Blaine had also changed in ways she didn't know. That said, she seriously doubted that so much had changed that Grant had morphed into a murderer.

"Yes, I suppose. But what did you learn? Grant sounded panicked beyond belief. I guess I would be too—not understanding the language, the rules."

"The policeman I spoke with said that he had been arrested just outside of Spoleto. Something about Grant leaving a train. The train was going from Florence to Rome. Grant reported his wife missing an hour or so after they left Florence. Police boarded the train in Perugia and checked for her. His account was all over the place."

"Could she have accidentally gotten off at the wrong stop?"

"They thought of that. By the time they reached Spoleto, they had alerted police between Florence and Orvieto and all stops in between, in case she got off. Grant got off the train to look for her. That was three days ago."

"Three days! Why is he just calling now?" Finley took a sip of her coffee and looked over the rim at Max.

"Because they just decided to charge him with murder."

"Did the guy on the phone say how they reached that conclusion? How they went from 'my wife is missing' to 'you must have killed her'? That's a pretty big jump."

"He didn't go into too much detail, but that is what they're now thinking."

Finley shook her head and shrugged in disbelief. "And what are we supposed to do?"

"I must admit, I'm a little baffled as to why he called you."

"That makes two of us." Finley rubbed her cup against her lower lip as she thought.

"How did he even know where to find you?"

"I guess he thought of anyone he knew in Europe, and we came to mind. The number he dialed was my old US WhatsApp, which I haven't used in years. A shot in the dark, I suppose. He was surprised the number still worked."

"So what are you going to do now? I have the address of the police station in Spoleto. They don't have a body or a weapon, so they are still investigating. But as far as they are concerned, they have a theory and a suspect."

"Now I understand why he was panicked. While we think this over, can we find food? I'm hungry." Finley grabbed the coffee cups and walked over to the sink.

Max intercepted her as she opened the dishwasher to deposit the rinsed cups. He pulled her to him. "Yes, we will feed you. And then we need to figure out how to extricate you from this thankless situation."

The walk up the lane to the high street was a short one, a few steps to Canterbury Arms, one of their favorite pubs. Finley remembered passing it the first time she had visited Max in London. It had been just after an eventful trip to Jaipur during which David and Whitt had gotten engaged, her dear friend Logan had met Hema, who was soon to be his wife, and she and Max had almost lost each other forever. Instead of splitting up, however, they had reconciled and cemented their relationship.

They chose a table in the garden with a smattering of sun, taking advantage of the warm day, which had also been blessed with cooling breezes. Once they had perused the late-lunch specials and ordered, they returned to the earlier conversation.

"Did they tell you why they switched from thinking she was missing to being sure that she's dead?" Finley took a sip of the South African Chenin Blanc.

"Nope. I suspect they looked for her, couldn't find her, and cooked up a nice story about him getting rid of his wife to go live with his mistress in Portofino."

Finley's eyes widened. "Is that what the policeman said?"

"No, sweetheart! I'm making this up, but I don't think it's far from the truth." Max shook his head. "The officer communicated only bits of information, most of it unclear, except for the name and location of the station."

"Then we'll have to get the facts from Grant when we get there." Finley said as she leaned back to let the waiter place her eggs Benedict on the table in front of her.

Max waited until the server left before he spoke, his eyebrow raised in question. "So you're going to Italy? To do what?"

"To see if we can help," Finley replied, taking a bite of her food. "We can't just leave him there!"

"Um, I see." Max sat looking at her for a few moments.

Finley sensed that he wanted to say more so she waited.

Max shifted in his seat. "I don't know how to say this, so excuse me if it comes out wrong, but I need to ask." He paused again.

"Max, darling, what is it you want to know? Something about this is making you uncomfortable, so just say it."

"Are there unresolved feelings for Grant that are prompting you to go to his rescue?"

Finley sat forward in surprise before recovering herself and responding. "No, dearest, there are no unresolved feelings. And surely not after a decade. Whatever was between Grant and me is long over. It was over before the divorce was finalized."

"So, you are telling me that you would rush across the continent for me, even if we hadn't seen each other since our first encounter in Morocco?"

"Yes, if you were in trouble."

"Even after I'd hurt you?" Max caught her eye and held it.

Finley softened her gaze and laid her hand over his. "Yes. Even then, if you had called, I would have come to your aid. I loved you."

Max took a swig of his wine and held it before swallowing hard. "That is what I'm afraid of."

"That I still love Grant?" Finley's voice was soft. "No. I love only you. But I did spend a long time loving him as his girlfriend and then as his wife before you came into my life. We parted for a lot of reasons, one of which was that we stopped loving each other."

"Okay. But you must admit how *irregular* this looks." Max stabbed at his spinach feta omelet while giving her a sideways glance.

She could see that he was not convinced. "However strange it may seem to you, I don't know what else to do. How would you feel if you were in Grant's situation and the person you called for help simply threw up their hands and walked away?"

"First of all, I would have been more judicious in whom I called, and secondly, I would have been more explicit in what I wanted them to do." Max took a bite but then stopped chewing to watch her reaction.

"I doubt you would have thought it all out that clearly if you'd been on holiday with me and were suddenly accused of murdering me," Finley replied. "Going from asking them to help find me to being dragged into a cell, facing the noose."

"Well, Italy doesn't have the death penalty, but I get your point."

"I know you think a trip would be a fool's folly, but my gut says it's the right thing to do," Finley said as she passed the rest of her eggs Benedict over for Max to finish. "The best way to settle it is to put it to the court of Mama."

For the rest of their meal and the leisurely walk home, Finley and Max talked about mundane things—getting new cushions for the patio furniture and an article in the *Times* on new car models that might be offered later in the year. Finley suggested they take the long way back to the house, putting her arm in Max's as she turned to take the path that cut through another row of mews houses before opening onto a green that skirted the back side of their property. It allowed them both time to think.

When they reached home, Max pulled Finley's phone from her bag and passed it to her. "Call your mother. I'm curious about what she'll say."

"I know what she'll say. 'Go help the boy out,'" Finley said assuredly. "And Daddy'll agree."

Max shook his head. "No way. But whatever their response, will you do what they say? If they say butt out, will you back off and leave it alone?"

"I will ask Daddy to find him a good lawyer, and that will be that."

"That will be the extent of your involvement?"

"That will be all." Finley leaned over to kiss him gently. "But if Mama says we need to go, will you likewise abide by her advice?"

Max pulled her closer and kissed her firmly. "Yes, I too will abide. Goodness, I feel like a preacher's son with all this *abiding*."

Finley wasn't surprised when Mama picked up on the first ring and turned her camera around so that both she and Daddy were in the frame. "I'd been waiting for you! I just spoke to your sister—and David, of course. They seem to be doing well, even with all the moving around."

"Hi, Mama. Daddy." Finley responded, adjusting the phone on the stand so that Max could be seen. "Yeah, Max and I talked to them yesterday. I wanted her to bring some Georgian wine when they come this way for Logan and Hema's wedding this summer."

"I am *so* excited for them. Odessa was a bit put out when she got her invitation."

"What? Upset that she didn't snag Logan herself?"

"Of course, darling! What else?"

Finley chuckled at her cousin Odessa, a bighearted Southern woman with an equally large personality who had rarely met a handsome man she hadn't liked. She especially appreciated the men that Whitt and Finley had chosen as their partners as well as the others they had brought around to Mama and Daddy's house over the years. Logan Reynolds had been one of those men who was very FOF—fond of Finley—until Max turned up, and Logan found Hema.

"Speaking of men on Odessa's list, guess who called today?" Finley caught Max's eye as she spoke. "Grant!"

"Grant, your ex-husband?" It was Daddy who spoke this time. He had never particularly liked Grant. Always thought he was a little stuck up. "Was there something he needed after all this time?"

Finley cleared her throat. "Yes, as matter of fact, there was. He needed help. He's in jail. In Italy."

"What in goodness's name?" Mama drew back from the screen, her hand moving to her chest. "What is he charged with? Drunkenness? Reckless driving? Whatever it is, you have to help him get out."

"Murder. Of Blaine, his wife." Finley waited for their reaction.

Mama's eyes widened, and her hand moved from her chest to mouth and back again. "Murder? That's absurd. That boy may be a lot of things, but a murderer he ain't. He just doesn't have it in him."

"I'd have to agree. I never liked him much. More pomp than circumstance, but I wouldn't think he's capable of murder." Daddy scowled. "Does he have a decent lawyer? How'd you find out all this?"

"As to the lawyer, I don't really know. I don't think so. On the finding out, I was his one call! Max talked to the policeman."

"What did the police say?" Daddy asked, engaging Max through the screen.

"Not much, just that Grant and his wife had been traveling in Italy, he had reported her missing, and that they now think he killed her, pushed her off the train. He's being held over in Spoleto."

Daddy was quiet for a few moments, and Finley and her mama held their tongues while he thought. "Can you get to him, girl?"

Finley turned to look at Max, who had failed to mask the surprise on his face. "Yes, we can fly over. I don't have anything pressing to submit right now, and I think Max is in the same boat."

"Yes, you must go help that poor boy out!" Mama said. "You may be divorced, but he's still family! His mother and I still exchange cards each Christmas."

Max took himself out of the camera frame and stared at Finley incredulously. He kept shaking his head in disbelief.

"I don't ever get a card," Finley grumbled.

Her mother tsked. "That would be too strange and might put her at odds with the new wife. You have to consider these things. Does his mother know?"

Finley was quick to respond. "No. And I wouldn't suggest you tell her. I think he called me rather than someone in the States because I was relatively nearby and because I'm unlikely to know anyone in his current circle. He hasn't even called the embassy."

There was another lag in the conversation that Finley—and now Max—knew she had to wait out. Mama and Daddy would decide the direction she would follow, and Max would abide.

2

IN THE SHORT TIME SINCE Finley's conversation with her parents, things had moved quickly. Daddy had contacted a former colleague of his living in Rome, looking for a good defense attorney to represent Grant. In the meantime, Finley had started reading up on the Italian legal system, which significantly differed from that of the United States. For one thing, the Italians didn't have the option of bail. The accused had to stay in jail until the trial was over. Grant would be held until then.

Max had sat stunned for the first few hours after the call. Finley's father had never been shy about expressing his clear dislike of Grant. That was what seemed so surprising about the sudden rally in support of Finley's ex-husband.

"Confused?" Finley asked. She climbed onto his lap and gave him a hug. "You have to understand the Southern code of justice."

Max looked at her askance. "What do you mean? Vigilantism?"

"That's a stereotype! 'Grab the shotgun and render your own verdict!' No, it's more subtle than that."

"Enlighten me."

They had switched from afternoon tea to wine and were curled up on the sofa in the den, thinking about the situation. Finley had tried to read, trusting that her father would text her as soon as he had any further news, but found little to distract her in the words on the page. Max had pulled out his computer and was looking at flight options.

"It's pretty basic," Finley explained. "Southerners can fight like cats and dogs within the unit, whether that be a family, a clutch of neighborhood women, the old boys' network, whatever. But as soon as there is an outside threat, all slights are forgotten—or at least put aside—and they close ranks to protect their own."

Max's lips curled into a smirk. "So, Grant may have been persona non grata at any Blake family event, but as extended—even expired—family, he gets the full protection plan when faced with the prospect of an Italian jail?"

"Yep. That pretty much sums it up." Finley grinned. "Northerners do the same thing. You just are more exclusive as to who gets into the tent in the first place."

"So, your parents think there is nothing unusual about sending you to 'help the boy out,' as your mother said."

Finley shook her head. "Nothing at all. And that was my first instinct. You were the only thing causing me to check my sanity. And I still want to be sure you're okay with this."

"I am, sweetheart, but I *do* find it odd," he said before she rose from his lap and he returned to checking flight availability for the next couple of days.

Finley was in her upstairs office laying out her camera equipment when Max stuck his head around the door.

"What's up? You have that look in your eye." Finley tilted her head slightly to get a full view of his face.

"And what look is that?" Max asked suggestively with a sly smile.

"Stop it. You know what I mean. Your 'come hither' look is different. This is a 'I know we said it was settled but . . .' look. What are you thinking?"

"I know I said I would 'abide,' follow whatever your mother said was best, but . . ."

"Mama and Daddy both said we need to see what we can do to help. What are you concerned about?" she asked softly.

"That we are walking into something we know nothing about. We have only partial facts of what happened. We don't know the legal structure or what is possible. And . . ." Max stopped speaking and moved closer to Finley before continuing.

"And we don't really know much about Grant. It has been ten years since you last had more than a passing conversation with him. A lot changes in that time."

"I don't disagree, but I also don't think a person changes that much."

"Maybe, but we don't know the circumstances, the nature of Grant and his wife's relationship, the events leading up to this."

"No, we don't, but that's what we are going to find out." Finley got up and went to stand beside Max. "If you really feel uncomfortable about this, I can go alone."

"No way. I'm going with you!" Max paused. "But would you humor me? Can we get a second opinion?"

Finley was curious now. "Of course, but whom are you thinking of?"

"Evans."

Finley stifled a laugh and struggled to mask her surprise. "Evans? You want to talk to Evans?"

She thought back over the several years they had known Chief Inspector Gareth Evans, a white-collar crime specialist at Interpol. Max often had resisted Evans's involvement, indeed his very presence.

"I know. But he may be able to help us understand Grant's situation better and maybe get us some inside information that will help."

Finley pulled Max closer and kissed his cheek. "I know you're trying to make the best of this highly unusual situation. Yes, we can call Evans."

She pulled out her phone and scrolled her contacts for Evans's number. When she found his name, she passed the phone to Max.

"What? You want me to ask?" Max's eyes widened as he stared at Finley's extended hand and the phone she held.

Finley raised a brow and thrust the phone closer. "You're the one with the question. Not me."

Max shook his head and chuckled. "The man is going to think I've gone insane. I'm not sure I can even recall all the facts."

"You'll remember. There aren't many," Finley said as she watched Max cautiously push the call button, still eyeing the phone like it was a snapping turtle that might rear up and bite him.

As the call rang through, Finley observed her partner. A reserved man with a logical mind, Max was loath to get involved in Grant's dilemma and abhorred even more the thought of drawing Evans into the morass. That he had agreed to call was evidence of his strong desire to free himself—and her—from whatever trouble there was.

"Hello?" Evans's resonant British baritone vibrated through the mike.

"Evans? This is Max. Finley's husband."

Finley had gotten over her initial reluctance to being called his wife when they were not actually married. But now, having settled into her relationship with him in a way that could only be described as husband and wife, she rather liked the sound of him declaring himself as her husband.

Before Max could continue, Evans jumped in. "Max, is everything all right? Finley! Has something happened?"

"No. No. Everything's fine. Finley is well. She's standing right here. I'll pass the phone over in a bit so you can catch up." Max hurried through the explanation to preempt another interruption. "Look, I had a question for you."

Max briefly recounted the call from Grant earlier in the day and the brief conversation with the Italian police officer. "What's your take? Finley and her parents are ready to hop on a plane and rally the troops. I don't know enough to say one way or the other."

With that, Finley took the phone from Max and put it on speaker so she too could hear his response. Both she and Max waited while Evans pondered his answer.

"This is pretty serious. From what little you have told me, the police have narrowed down the field of suspects in the last few days and have settled on Grant. And you said they haven't found a body or any sort of weapon that might have been used?"

"Nothing as far as we know. Just a missing woman."

"Were any clothes or other items missing?"

"Nope. Nothing was mentioned. The impression I got was that all of her things were left on the train. She just disappeared."

Evans went quiet again. Finley could imagine his hawklike brow puckering and releasing as he thought through the scant facts of the case.

"Bother! This is a tough one. I wish I could get there to help you, but I am out in the field. A good ten thousand miles from you. I won't be back that way for a few weeks, and by that time, he may be convicted and sentenced."

"That quickly? I thought the Italian courts would be glacially slow," Max said.

"They might be, but with what they think is an open-and-shut case, they are going to try to close it out as quickly as possible. In that case, it would be only the appeal that would go slowly. He could be in jail for years before the appeal was even heard."

Both sides were silent with that dire news.

Max broke the silence. "What do you suggest, then? If conviction is a forgone conclusion, is there anything to be done?"

"Keep them from convicting him! You're going to have to conduct the investigation that the police will never do. They have their man. You have to gather enough evidence to make them doubt that conclusion," Evans said emphatically. "Do you speak Italian?"

"Yes. It's passable. Enough for us to ask some basic questions and start to raise doubts."

"Good. Get there as soon as you can, hire a skilled lawyer who won't cower under police directives, and start rattling cages! I'm sure Finley and Whitt are up to the task," Evans laughed.

In the three years he had known the sisters, he had pulled their tushes out of the fire innumerable times. That hadn't stopped them from going in the next time, hellbent on getting to the truth. Their tenacity—and their ability to bring killers to justice—was to be admired.

"Guess you answered my question. Finley's feeling vindicated. She and her mother are determined to see him freed. I suppose I have no choice but to help their cause."

Evans gave throaty laugh. "Good man! Never challenge a woman on a mission—especially when she is backed up by her mother. I really am sorry I can't be of more help."

"This has been quite useful. Are you reachable if we have more questions once we arrive in Spoleto?"

"Certainly. Always on this number. Finley knows," Evans confirmed. "Now, let me hear your lovely wife's voice!"

While Finley finished her companionable chat with Evans, Max returned to his study downstairs. She found him with his head bent over his computer and could hear the quiet whirr of the printer.

"What're you printing?" Finley picked up one of the pages and saw it was a list of tomorrow's flights to Italy.

"I concede. You win. I will abide. Evans confirmed it. We have to go."

"Well, I'm glad you're feeling better about this. Evans's assessment was pretty scary, though. When are we leaving?"

"I'm trying to figure out the best way to get there. Via Perugia is closer, but Rome is faster and cheaper." Max pointed to the map on his screen. "And we need to find someplace to stay."

"I'm sure we can find an Airbnb near Spoleto. There are quite a few small towns nearby. I know we can find something if we aren't wedded to being right in the city. In fact, I would prefer it."

Max was still looking at the map as the last of the pages came off the printer. "Pettino. I know that town. It's truffle country. A friend of mine from New York bought a truffle farm near there a few years ago. Maybe we can stay nearby. It would be nice to catch up with him. And he might be able help us with the context. What time is it there?"

"They're only an hour ahead. While you call, I'll pour us another glass of something. Would you prefer more wine or bubbly this time? Or maybe a single malt?"

"Wine, if you don't mind. I liked the merlot we just had. Nice and smooth."

"Merlot it is, then." Finley slipped down the hall to the kitchen and came back several minutes later with a tray that held the red wine for Max and a glass of prosecco for her, as well as a plate of pecorino and aged Parmesan.

Max was on the phone when she walked back in. "Well, we don't want to put you out. We don't know how long this is going to take."

Finley listened as he finished the call. She took her flute of prosecco and a piece of Parmesan dipped in syrupy, aged balsamic over to the oversize leather armchair that occupied a sizeable part of the study's sitting area. She watched Max as a winning smile claimed his face and a heartfelt laugh escaped his lips. His eyes diverted to her and crinkled mischievously as they settled on her observing him.

"Love you," he mouthed. He raised his glass.

Finley smiled and answered his salute. She took a sip of the prosecco. The sparkling wine was crisp and clean with an impressive show of tiny bubbles. *Not bad for a chance buy! Worth buying again.*

"Chuck, great talking to you, and thanks so much for the offer. Let me confirm it with Finley, and I'll text you within the hour. Looking forward to catching up regardless." Max took a quick sip of his wine as he listened to the reply from the other end of the line. "Take care. We'll see you tomorrow."

Max rose from his desk and came over to Finley. He sat on the wide arm of the chair and leaned over for a kiss. "Thanks for the wine. I really like this one."

"I do too."

"Are you drinking red? I thought I saw you with champagne."

"Yes, a nice prosecco, but I tasted the red on your lips, and it was very nice."

Max's lips slid up to give a lopsided grin. "Are you sure? Perhaps you need another taste."

Finley welcomed the kiss, wrapping one arm around him while holding her prosecco in the other. When they finished, she pronounced, "My opinion stands. It is an excellent red, enhanced by your luscious lips."

"I concur wholeheartedly." Max moved to the matching chair a few steps away. "It appears we have a place to stay."

"How did that come about?"

"My friend Chuck offered immediately. He was excited about the chance to catch up, and to meet you! We used to be good friends when I was in New York. He and his wife visited when I was in Tangier and here in London, in fact." Max sank farther into the seat and savored the wine. "A nice guy. I think you'll like him. And he will love you!"

Finley gave Max a side eye. "Just because you do, doesn't mean everyone else will. In any event, did you tell him why we were coming?"

"Yes, but not in so many words. I figured it was better for a face-to-face conversation."

"You're probably right. How do you say over the phone that someone you know might be guilty of murder?"

MEET ME CURBSIDE ON THE *second ring outside portal number three,* the message from Chuck had said. *Parking this behemoth is a pain!*

Finley wondered what he was talking about. All the Italian cars she remembered were compact little things, well suited to the narrow streets and curving roads. Her wonder turned to understanding, however, when she and Max saw the hulking minivan outside airport arrivals.

They had decided to fly into Rome, even though the trip to Perugia airport would have been shorter for Chuck, who insisted on picking them up.

"And no need to rent a car. We have two extras just sitting around. You can use one of them," Chuck had said.

So Max and Finley had surrendered themselves to Chuck and Sofia, his wife. Finley knew that Chuck and Max's friendship must have been something special. Despite his usual need for control, Max hadn't objected to any of Chuck's suggestions and had readily handed over the reins to him.

When the flight touched down shortly after 1:00 p.m., Finley and Max had already been up for over six hours. To add to Finley's misery, adrenaline and dread had combined to make the night sleepless. So when she dragged herself off the two-hour flight, she was listless and sleepy.

The staggeringly beautiful countryside and Chuck's running commentary on the history of the region kept her awake, however. That, and her prime seat beside him up front.

"Hope you don't mind, Max, but I want this pretty lady to have the best seat in the house," Chuck said as he pulled away from the curb.

He was a ruggedly attractive man, a decade older than Max, as Finley recalled. He was well maintained for his age, athletically fit from what she could see, but his features lacked the symmetry that would define him as handsome. Instead, he possessed a bravado that would put him clearly in the dashing category. He was Gerard Butler to Max's Patrick Dempsey.

"I think this is some of the most gorgeous countryside in the world. Everyone flocks to Tuscany, which is pretty, don't get me wrong. But there's something about Umbria that had my heart from the first time I visited."

"When was that? Have you been coming here long?" Finley asked.

"Over twenty years ago. Shortly after I met Sofia. She's from Assisi. And yes, that is a real town with real people." Chuck laughed. "As Sofia is fond of saying, the town existed long before Saint Francis was ever born. But she will acknowledge that he kind of put it on the map."

"How did you get into truffle farming?" Max leaned forward in his seat so he hung over Finley's shoulder. She reached up and gently touched his hand. He kissed her fingers in reply.

"We bought the land shortly after we got married. No real plan for what to do with it. We knew it was in prime truffling territory, but it had lain fallow for the longest," Chuck said as he shifted gears.

Finley noticed that he used gears and levers in both his right and left hands to change gears. While she thought it unusual, she also thought the minivan itself was something out of steampunk, so the double-handed gears fit right in.

"It wasn't until a few years ago, when we decided to move here, that we had to figure out what to do with the property. Neighbors noted to us that we had more than a few trees on the property that were good for truffling."

"Did you know anything about it?" Max asked.

Chuck laughed hard this time. "Not a thing! We pulled Sofia's dad out of retirement—he had been a truffler for a while. He showed us the basics and got us started."

"What does it mean to be a truffler?" Finley was curious now. She knew that truffles cost a mint in grocery stores and restaurants, but she had no idea what it meant to have a truffle farm. *How do you farm a mushroom?*

"It's actually easier than you think. And a lot riskier than you know," Chuck explained. "There are a few varieties of truffles, both white and black ones. They like nippy, humid environments, so winter is generally the harvest season. If you want white ones, you have to go to the Piedmont. Around Pettino, we have only the black ones, mainly sweet winter ones, but I also have one that can come ready in early summer. So you may be able to go hunting with us while you're here." He glanced over at Finley and added, "If you have time, with all that's going on."

"We'll fill you in once we get to the house. There isn't much more to tell, to be honest," Max said.

Finley redirected the conversation. "I still don't understand how you farm these things."

"Sorry, I can go off on tangents sometimes, so you have to keep me on track." Chuck shifted again as they prepared to leave the highway. "Truffles are like subterranean mushrooms. They like to grow in the roots of certain trees a bit below the soil level. So, if you have the right trees and the right soil microclimate, you have a chance at getting truffles, but there's no guarantee. Hence the scarcity. Lots of folks like to keep the best sites a secret."

"Can you plant them or seed them? Where does the farming come in?" Max asked.

"Farming is really a misnomer since you really can't cultivate them. Some people dip the roots of young trees in spores, but it's a crapshoot, and it takes years. They just grow. We were lucky. We planted the right trees years ago when the land was fallow—not for truffling but to prevent erosion." Chuck turned to Finley again and gave her an endearing smile. "See? Just dumb luck."

"That has netted you a pretty penny, if this house is any indication," Max said as they pulled into a cypress-lined road that led to a two-story stone and stucco manor house and gardens.

"It is a beauty, isn't it?" Chuck looked at the house with pride. "But you should have seen it when we moved here. It was so bad, we rented a little cottage down the road for two years while it was being renovated."

Finley stepped out of the vehicle and looked up at the rustic stone walls and running roses that decorated the facade and the adjacent wall of the house. "Never in a million years would I have guessed it had been in shambles. It's stunning."

She turned to see Max holding the door open as Chuck swiveled in the front seat. He reached back and pulled a wheelchair from a compartment behind his seat. Without saying a word, Max started to open the chair and position it so Chuck could get in it.

"I'm still getting used to having to pull this damn thing out. Up until six months ago, I was still mobile," Chuck muttered under his breath. "ALS is a b . . . Sorry. Excuse my language."

Max chuckled as he closed the driver's door. "Excused. Can you make it?"

Chuck nodded as he wheeled the chair along the entry path.

"Then I'll help Finley with the bags," Max said as he opened the rear hatch.

"Did you know?" Finley whispered as she reached for her duffel and the shopping bag with the gift she had wrapped for Chuck and his wife.

Max shook his head sadly and took the duffel from her before grabbing his carry-on.

"Welcome! Or more appropriately, *benvenuti*! Hope you had a good flight. Probably an early start for you." A striking woman with impish dark eyes approached them. She was petite, almost a foot shorter than Max, with a long salt-and-pepper-colored braid draped over her shoulder.

She greeted both of her guests with kisses on both cheeks. "Come in! Come in! I'm Sofia, if Chuck hadn't mentioned. You probably don't remember me from the New York days."

"But I do, and from your visits to Tangier and London with Chuck a while ago." Max hugged her and stepped back to introduce Finley. "And this is my wife, Finley. She was also in New York at the time, but we weren't together then."

"Ah!" was all Sofia said. She reached for the bags that Max had set down in the entryway. "Your room is upstairs."

"Here, just point us in the right direction, and we can find it ourselves." Max took the bags from her and started up the steps. Finley followed.

"At the top of the stairs, to the right. We'll be on the terrace if you want to freshen up," Sofia called after them.

A few minutes later, Max and Finley joined Chuck and Sofia on a large stone expanse that offered a breathtaking view of the surrounding hills.

Finley stood at the threshold of the terrace and took in the view, a palette of every shade of green imaginable, dabbed here and there with terracotta and ochre from the houses that peeked out from behind the trees, then dotted with pricks of pink and red from oleander and geraniums. "If I lived here, I would never leave this space."

"Oh, yes, you would. Most of the rooms have this view or one like it." Chuck smiled. "Throw open your shutters upstairs and catch a glimpse. I think that room has the most spectacular panoramic view. That used to be our room."

"We're sorry. Did we put you out of your room?" Finley exclaimed. "We can take any of them."

Sofia held up her hand. "You didn't put us out of our room—"

"ALS did," Chuck interrupted her with a rueful smile. "I should have said something when we were on the phone. Sofia scolded me after I hung up."

"But what were you going to say? We've known each other long enough. You say what you want, when you want. I just wanted to see you. And Sofia. And to have you meet Finley." Max held his friend's gaze.

"We don't invite many people to visit. But something said you were the right ones to come here. My gut was on target," Chuck said, turning to Finley. "What can I offer you to drink? We have some great local Chianti. And some prosecco on ice!"

Finley smiled. "Did Max forewarn you about my sparking beverage addiction? I'll have the prosecco—but I'm going to steal a taste of Max's Chianti."

Once the wine was poured and local cheeses sampled, Chuck directed his gaze to Finley. "So, what has your former young man gotten himself into?"

"I really don't know. As Max probably told you, he called out of the blue, asking for help. He said he had been arrested for the murder of his wife. They'd been on a second honeymoon trip and were taking the train from Vienna to Rome. When he couldn't find her, he got off the train and contacted the police."

"And he just happened to get off near here?" Chuck asked.

"I guess so. So much is unclear. He only had a couple of minutes to talk. The rest Max got from one of the policemen who was there."

"They talked to you?"

"Yes, Grant passed him the phone at some point, and I started asking him questions in Italian. I think he forgot whom he was talking to when he heard the Italian and started sharing what he knew, which again wasn't much. We're scheduled to speak with Grant tomorrow."

"Maybe you'll get more facts then. Sounds like a pretty tough one, especially if the police have settled on their man." Chuck didn't look convinced that much could be done.

However, Sofia's mention of food seemed to change the somber mood. "Well, for now, let's enjoy ourselves. We'll have a bit of lunch and then a rest—it's a tradition that must not be broken! And tonight, some neighbors are coming over. They are bringing their wine, and we are sharing our truffles!"

After a sumptuous lunch of dried meats, roast chicken, cheese, pickled vegetables, and bread, Finley was ready for a nap. While she surmised that the rest was built into the schedule to accommodate Chuck's needs, she was glad for the chance to stretch out and maybe catch a bit of much-needed sleep.

"I got a message from Daddy. The attorney he found said he contacted Grant, but Grant said Blaine's parents had arranged one for him." She scanned her messages as she sat on the edge of the bed.

"One less thing we need to bother with, then."

"I suppose it is a little odd for your ex-wife's parents to hire a lawyer for you."

"Finally, you're coming around to understanding how really *strange* this whole situation is."

"Maybe for those of you with Yankee reserve. For us Southerners, it is as natural as breathing." Finley straightened her shoulders in good Southern girl fashion and shot Max a look before reclining on the carved four-poster bed. "We look after one another."

Max came over to her resting place on the bed and kissed her cheek. "I will remember that. I will make it my quest, fair fragile maid, to look after you so that no harm comes to you."

Finley pushed him off with a grin. "You've missed the point completely."

Max smirked gleefully as he went around to the other side of the bed and claimed his place. Both of them lay staring out over the countryside. Chuck hadn't done the view justice when he'd described it earlier.

Finley had thrown open the shutters when they'd come up for their rest and had frozen in awe midswing. The view from below offered a slice of the terrain, but upstairs, the rolling hills mixed with alternating green and brown plains that stretched for miles. Church towers reached skyward, surrounded by patches of terracotta and green, giving definition to the little towns and villages that punctuated the landscape. A dusty haze had settled in places as the sun started to cast afternoon shadows.

"I could get used to this," Max murmured as he reached for Finley's hand.

"You sound like David," Finley said. Her brother-in-law made the same observation each time he was in a luxurious setting, whether it be in Jaipur, Charleston, or Palawan.

"Is he wrong? Wouldn't you like this as a lifestyle?" Max gazed over at Finley as he held her hand. "Gorgeous scenery, great food, lazy afternoons, and evenings enjoying the company of friends over wine and more good food? Not a bad life."

"No, it isn't, but I'm not ready to slow down this much just yet. I like our traveling and adventures. Even when we get into tight spots."

"Another thing to keep in mind. You are a fountain of revelations today."

"Stop teasing and let me get some sleep before dinner."

Dinner was on the back terrace, where the late lunch had been. By the time Finley and Max came downstairs, several of the guests had arrived.

"So sorry, we didn't know we were late," Finley said as she walked into the group that was already well into their first glass of wine.

"You're not late at all. We don't stand on ceremony, as the British say. Amata brought over a couple of new wines and olive oils that we hadn't tried before, and we decided to get an early start," Sofia explained. She offered Max and Finley a choice of red or white from glasses already poured and introduced Amata and her husband, Silvano, as a vintner and restauranteur, respectively.

"Let me introduce you around." Chuck turned to an older couple seated on a bench that overlooked the hills. "This is Mario and Elena Fuscati. Veteran truffle farmers who live next door. And Gary and Pierre, who live down the road. Gary is an artist, and Pierre is a retired diplomat."

"And here come the stragglers," Sofia teased.

"We are perennially late to whatever event. I think I have a late gene," the woman offered.

"My sister says the same thing. She also has the shopping gene!" Finley kidded while offering her hand. "Finley Blake. This is my husband, Max."

The woman, whom Finley would have labeled as French even before she spoke, was dressed in white jeans and a black, light-weight, V-necked sweater that she had cinched with an embroidered Turkish belt and accessorized with a chunky, hammered collar necklace and flawless makeup.

"Oktavia Martin," she announced in accented English as she turned to the man who had accompanied her. "And my husband, Laurent."

With introductions done and drinks passed, the party broke into clusters of conversation on the mix of wrought-iron chairs, rattan love seats, and Moroccan cushions scattered about the elegant terrace. Chuck and Mario were regaling Max with accounts of the biggest tubers they had found. Laurent and Oktavia were catching Sofia, Gary, and Pierre up on the latest art news from

Paris, having just seen an exhibition of digital art in the Marais. Elena and Amata were comparing truffle recipes.

"I find the hardest to deal with are the white ones, if you can ever find them," Elena was saying as Finley joined the group.

"Excuse my ignorance, but why are the white ones harder to cook?" Finley asked.

"Oh, you don't cook them! They're too delicate. Which is why handling them is harder," Elena explained as they settled in on a love seat.

Amata took a sip of her wine and looked at Finley before she spoke. "Enough about recipes. So, Chuck said that you were here to help a friend who's in trouble."

Elena leaned in, unable to hide her curiosity.

Finley smiled. "Yes. My ex-husband, to be exact. Arrested for the alleged murder of his wife."

"Why do you say *alleged*?" Elena was all ears now.

"Because there is no body and no murder weapon," Finley said.

There was a pregnant pause as all three women took another sip of their wine and looked out over the countryside.

"Maybe she isn't really dead," Amata said somewhat hesitantly.

Finley stared at the woman in shock, pondering the possibility before giving a delayed response. "Maybe you're right."

RICH FOOD AND COPIOUS AMOUNTS of wine slowed Max and Finley's rise the next morning. As much as they would have liked to sleep in, they were scheduled to meet with Grant at nine o'clock.

"What would you like to drink with your breakfast? I know you're rushing off to the jailhouse, but Sofia has breakfast all ready for you." Chuck was waiting for them on the terrace when they came down. He was out of his wheelchair and sitting on a wide wooden barrel chair with a high bottom and sturdy arms, a majolica cup in hand.

Sofia came onto the terrace with a pot in each hand. "Good morning. Before you hurry off, take time to grab a coffee and some food. You don't know when you are going to eat again."

"The woman has the need to feed, so please indulge her." Chuck pointed at the sumptuous spread on the sideboard. "Help yourselves."

"Have you already eaten?" Finley asked, eyeing his cup.

Chuck nodded. "I'm normally up at five in the morning. A holdover from my trading days."

Finley recalled that Max had said Chuck had been a commodities trader before switching to foreign exchange during the time they had been in New York. He continued to trade remotely in his semiretirement.

Max grabbed a plate. "Well, I'm not going to let this magnificent smorgasbord go uneaten! You'll have to tell me what we have here."

Sofia set the pots of coffee and warmed milk down at the end of the table and then came to join him at the sideboard. "Let's see. You have all of the usual things—breads and some jams from local fruit. And the olive oil Amata brought last night—we use that instead of butter. Try it. It adds a nice nutty flavor."

Finley sliced off a piece of bread and drizzled it with oil before adding a thick slice of ham.

"The ham is from a farm not far from here that makes a wide range of sausages as well as hams. Maybe I'll get some sausages for tomorrow's breakfast," Sofia added. "If you want, I can make you some eggs. I collected them from the coop this morning."

Finley heard Max draw in a breath. She knew what he was going to say before he said it. Like a kid looking for a second helping, he asked sheepishly, "Might I get an egg lightly scrambled? I am a sucker for fresh eggs."

Chuck held out his cup. "And might I get a bit more coffee with some of the warmed milk you brought out?"

"If you'll allow me, I'll get your coffee while Sofia gets Max's egg," Finley suggested as Sofia nodded and headed into the kitchen. Finley carried the pots of coffee and milk over to Chuck, looking puzzled when he asked her to pour out a measure of milk first and then coffee.

He gave a wry smile as he observed her curiosity. "You're wondering why I didn't do the coffee first and then the milk, eh?"

Finley nodded as she watched the two blend together.

"If I put the milk in first and then the coffee, I don't have to balance a spoon to do the stirring!" Chuck took a sip. "It's already stirred. One less thing I have to drop!"

"Stop feeling sorry for yourself," Sofia teased as she came back into the room with Max's eggs. "You can always drink it black and make it simpler still."

"You see how she torments me!" Chuck countered with feigned distress before he changed the subject. "You're going to love our little jailhouse."

Sofia shook her head. "He's being facetious. It's housed in an old mansion in the center of town. Beautiful stone-arched building. Chuck says it matches the efficiency of the police. They're better at sipping espresso or grappa on the terrace than they are at catching criminals."

"Well, they seem to think they have caught one with Grant," Finley said.

"Do you think he did it?" Chuck looked up from his coffee, staring at her intently while she pondered the question.

"No. I haven't seen him in a decade, but I don't think he's a killer." Finley paused. *But people do change.*

"Finley! Thank God you came!" Grant said, knocking over the chair as he rose. The guard, startled by the sound of the chair hitting the floor, rushed over to their table. Finley raised her hand instinctively to warn him off. He gave her a stern look before returning to his position against the wall.

"Grant. How are you? I'm so sorry you're in this position." Finley hesitated, not knowing how to greet him—with a kiss or a handshake. She resolved her dilemma by quickly taking the seat across from him as Max pulled up an extra chair. "This is my husband, Max. You two may have met in New York. We had some of the same friends."

The two men exchanged handshakes with little more than a nod. Finley could tell they were sizing each other up. Max clearly had the upper hand. Not only was he Finley's current to Grant's ex, but he also wasn't garbed in drab, high-water prison scrubs with a day-old scruff on his chin. Grant looked like Gulliver sitting at the small wooden conference table, his tall, gangly frame almost folded in two. Still, he was the ever-stoic man she remembered from all those years ago.

"I'm holding up. The food isn't bad, the conditions are pretty clean, and they let me see my lawyer whenever I want. Not that that seems to help."

"Are you not satisfied with your attorney?" Max asked.

"If not, Daddy has one that he found through friends," Finley added.

"No, no need. Blaine's parents secured one for me immediately after I called them. After I spoke to you, I decided to call them to let them know that Blaine was missing. I thought maybe they could hire someone to find her since I was trapped in here."

"Good thinking." Mindful of the limited time they might be allowed together, Finley shifted in her chair before opening her questioning. Her probing wasn't going to be comfortable for any of those present. "Can you tell me again what happened? From the very beginning. And please, don't leave anything out, even if it's painful. It might be important."

Grant sighed deeply. "This was supposed to be our second honeymoon. Ten years, can you believe it?"

He paused, his mouth twisting as he pondered his next thought. Finley could see he was considering what to share. Finley was his ex-wife, after all. She decided to help him along.

"Were you happy?"

Grant's brow puckered and then relaxed. "We've had our ups and downs, like any married couple. But we've stuck together, at times for the sake of the children. Two little girls, six and a half and four."

Finley smiled at the thought of the two little blondes who would likely mirror Grant's heavy flaxen curls, dazzling smile, and deep-set blue eyes. "And most recently, things were good?"

"Yes. Very good." Grant grinned slightly. "The trip, the time away, it was just what we needed."

"So, describe the trip for me. Where did you start? Where did you go? When did you leave the States? Everything." Finley was probing, looking for anything that might tell her whether she was talking to a friend or a murderer.

"We left the States almost three weeks ago now. The girls spend the summer with their grandparents each year, so we decided to take advantage of that to make this a real anniversary."

"Where did you start?" Max asked again.

"Paris. Then we flew to Vienna. Stayed there almost a week, and then we headed to Rome. I booked the overnight train that passed through both Venice and Florence but arranged it so we could get off and explore if we wanted to. We followed the plan until we got to Florence."

"What happened in Florence?" Finley leaned forward in interest.

Before Grant could continue, Max interrupted. "Can you lay out the overall plan first? Then we can get to the deviation."

Finley smiled. Max wanted to see the full scope before they narrowed in. She, on the other hand, went for the detail and then tried to lace together the pieces. In that way, they were perfect complements.

Grant outlined the initial tour itinerary. "From Vienna, we were to take the train to Florence and then to Rome. We had both been to Venice and Florence before but hadn't spent much time in Rome, so we were going to focus there."

"So, you got on the train in Vienna. At what time?" Max had pulled out a small notebook.

Grant detailed the train schedule and his and Blaine's movements from the time they got on the train until he noticed her missing.

"We got off in Florence to stretch our legs, and then we both got back on." Grant closed his eyes. "I drifted off to sleep at some point shortly after. Blaine wasn't there when I woke up a time later. I didn't think anything of it initially."

"When did you start to get concerned?" Finley watched Grant's face for any sign of dissembling or equivocation but saw none when he responded.

"It was just before we pulled into Perugia. I had walked the length of the train, and when we stopped, I scanned the platform looking for her. I thought maybe she had gone to the bar car and exited from there, that we had just missed each other. She liked getting off to stretch whenever we stopped."

"But you still didn't see her on the platform?" Max asked. Finley noticed that he bit his lip as he waited for Grant's answer. She wondered what other question he had really wanted to ask.

Grant shook his head. "I alerted one of the conductors when I got back on. When we got to Orvieto, I asked him to help me get our bags off."

"Why did you get off?" Finley was confused and somewhat incredulous at Grant's decision to leave the train.

"They had helped me search the train for her once we left Perugia. We looked everywhere. I thought she had decided to do her own thing and head to Assisi."

Finley and Max traded glances before Finley asked the question that seemed to have popped into both of their minds. "What does Assisi have to do with anything?"

"We had argued earlier in the day about doing a side trip to Assisi. She wanted to jump off, and I wanted to get to Rome. She was quite huffy about it," Grant confided.

"Enough that you thought she might have gotten off the train and headed there without you?" Max's inflection told everything. He didn't believe Grant—at all.

Finley attempted to deflect from the incredulousness that underlay Max's question. "Would she have gotten off without taking her bags?"

Grant sat back and sighed. "You don't believe me either. The police asked the same questions. I don't know what to say besides what was going through my mind."

Finley gave him a sympathetic smile. "It was that big of a blowout, eh?"

Grant chuckled and nodded. "I wasn't thinking clearly, so I figured she wasn't either. I just decided to take the next train to Assisi. To follow her, so I thought." He leaned in closer. "But I can't share any of this with the police. It just makes me seem more guilty than not."

Finley had been deep in thought much of the way back to the farm, and Max hadn't interrupted. Instead, he concentrated on navigating the little Fiat 500 that Chuck had lent them around the curvy roads connecting Spoleto to the surrounding villages.

When they pulled onto the tree-lined road that led to the house, Max laid his hand on Finley's. "Are you okay?"

"It looks pretty bad, doesn't it?" Her eyes were fixed in front of her, her lips pressed together.

Max grunted in the affirmative.

She looked over at him and sighed. "I suppose you're right. Now that we're here and the facts are laid out, I'm just wondering whether there's anything we can really do to change the outcome of this whole situation."

"Perhaps not, but you never know unless you try," Max said as he slid out of the car. "And you Blake women have never been quitters. I think Grant knows that. It's probably why he called."

Finley greeted him with a loving kiss when he came around to open her door.

"How did it go?" Sofia was standing in the entryway when they came in. She had a pitcher of something that looked like sangria in her hand. "Come join us. Amata and I are having an impromptu party! Chuck is napping before lunch, so we're drinking alone."

Finley kissed both of her cheeks. "We'll meet you outside after we freshen up. We could definitely use a drink!"

When she and Max came back down, Chuck was up from his nap and had a drink in hand. "Sofia has made some Italian sangria—hers has prosecco in it! I think it is better than that Spanish stuff, but I'm biased."

Sofia planted a kiss on his forehead and held the pitcher aloft. Both Finley and Max accepted a drink, greeted Amata with kisses, and took a seat on the chairs overlooking the hills. Finley took a sip of her drink before she answered the question that had been hanging in the air.

"To your earlier question of how it went, things don't look good for him." She recounted the facts that Grant had shared. "Something doesn't add up. Where did she go? Why did he get off? So many questions."

"You don't believe him?" Sofia asked softly.

Finley shrugged. "I don't know what to believe, frankly. I want to believe him, but there are gaps in what he's saying, things that don't make sense. Maybe I'm just too close to this to be objective."

Chuck turned to look at Max. "What do you think? Is he telling the truth?"

Max chuckled. "As far-fetched as some of this is, I almost have to believe it because no one would make something like this up."

Finley reached over to touch Max's hand. He had given her hope when she feared there was none.

Throughout the conversation, Amata had remained silent, taking periodic sips of her sangria. Now, she directed her gaze at Finley. "Do you think he killed her?"

Finley hesitated before she answered. "No. No, I don't, but it's a gut feeling. I don't have proof otherwise. There's no body, but there is also no Blaine to refute that a murder happened."

"Maybe, but if there's a body to be found, you'll find it. Grant's counting on it," Max said.

"That's the rub. To clear him, we have to find the body or the murder weapon and prove that someone else did it."

Amata stood and poured the others more sangria before topping off her glass. She paused before she spoke, enunciating each word carefully. "Unless, as I said before, she isn't dead."

5

A MATA'S COMMENT ERUPTED INTO A discussion that lasted the duration of lunch and a good while after. Her conclusion was that, however implausible it might be, given the evidence the police said they had, no one should assume Blaine was dead until there was a body.

"I'm not sure I follow your logic, Amata, dear." Chuck popped an olive from the antipasti into his mouth, even as he signaled to Sofia that he was finished eating. She slapped his hand lightly and shook her head vehemently as he reached for another one. He reluctantly conceded. "There are often accidents—or murders—where the body is never found, and yet someone is convicted."

Amata smiled knowingly. "I know, but all I'm saying is that we shouldn't assume she is dead just because we can't find a body."

"But what other options are there?" Chuck's voice rose in exasperation.

"Calm yourself, Chuck. She might have been in an accident and not had any ID with her. Or she might have fallen and have amnesia or have gotten lost and not have her phone. It has been only a few days."

"That last one may be a bit far-fetched. She could have borrowed one instead of letting her husband get arrested," Finley reasoned. "But I get where you are going with this. By jumping to the conclusion that she's dead, we—and the police—are narrowing the possibilities of what might have happened."

"And as a result, reducing the chance of finding her," Max concluded.

"Precisely," Amata confirmed.

"If that's the case, then we need to rethink all the evidence we have," Finley said. "Sofia, is there pen and paper we can use, please?"

While Sofia retrieved the paper and pen, Chuck sat scratching his head. "I still don't get why we're going down this rabbit hole. If you want to save Grant, you need to find someone else who might have wanted to kill her."

Finley divided the paper she was handed into two parts. At the top, she wrote *Dead* on one side and *Alive* on the other. "If she's dead, we need to look at the facts one way. If she is alive, then quite another."

"For example?" Chuck still looked confused.

"Let's start with what happened to the body. If she is dead, we've been asking where the body is or, more accurately, how did the body get off the train—" Finley said.

Max jumped in. "Since there was no body on the train, by all accounts."

"Right. So was it carried off? The police speculate that it was dumped off, but they concede that at no point along the tracks is there any indication of anything—body or junk—being dumped onto the embankment." Finley scribbled this information in the *Dead* column.

"But if she was alive, then we wouldn't have to figure out how she got off. She could have walked off!" Max was warming to the alternative approach to thinking the case through.

Amata nodded. "That is why, for me, until they find a body or a murder weapon—or even a murder scene—we have to allow for the possibility that she is still alive."

Chuck got ready to argue but lost energy before he could formulate the tenets of his response. "Still not convinced, but I am too tired to challenge you. Maybe after a nap."

Sofia took the handles of his chair and pointed him to his bedroom. After they had gone, Finley returned to the dual analysis.

"By assuming we're looking for a body, not a person, we've closed off the search for Blaine." She tapped the paper with her pen. "We've done the same thing the police did. They immediately directed their search to finding the killer—and once they focused on Grant, that was that. They didn't need to look any further."

"She could be anywhere by now!" Max threw up his hands. "It would be easy for her to take another train to wherever."

"Assuming she had means and a mode of transportation," Finley said.

"Do we know whether she had her purse?" Amata asked.

"I don't know. We didn't ask as many of those sorts of questions as we should have," Finley conceded sadly.

Max reached over and squeezed her shoulder. "Your first concern, as it should have been, was Grant's well-being."

Amata's simple question had opened a whole new line of inquiry that Finley hadn't considered. Blaine might still be alive. Even if she were dead, by at least looking for her, they were more likely to find her body. *Though, I hope for Grant's sake, she is still alive,* Finley thought as she and Max headed back to the police station for another conversation with Grant.

"If she's still alive, where do you think she could be?" Max asked as he drove the car up and down the undulating hills.

"I haven't the slightest. Which is what makes finding her so hard." Finely twisted her string belt around her finger before unwinding it and starting the twisting again. "Do you recall if Grant said Blaine was familiar with Italy?"

"I don't think she knew it that well. I got the impression that the two of them had been to some parts of Italy before but there was a lot they hadn't seen." Max glanced over at her. "That was why she was so dead set on going to Assisi."

"That's right. I had forgotten about her insistence on seeing Assisi. Amata's suggestion that she might be alive got me sidetracked."

"Maybe after we talk to Grant, we can take a quick trip to Assisi. I think it's only about thirty minutes from here."

Finley pulled out her phone and began studying a map of the region. "Yeah, Assisi isn't far. But when I look at the map, I'm confused. Grant said when he couldn't find her on the train, he got off thinking he would look for her in Assisi. But he didn't get off until Orvieto. That's a long way from Assisi. Or Perugia, for that matter."

Max shrugged. "Maybe it was an express?"

"Maybe." Finley frowned and returned to the map. "But the bigger question for me is, how did Grant end up in jail in Spoleto when he got off in Orvieto? What happened after he got off that train?"

"We'll have to ask him. I think we have a long list of questions for him."

Max pulled the car into a parking space off the main square. Before going to open Finley's door, he reached for her hand. "How are you holding up?"

She nodded. "As well as can be expected, I suppose. Every time I ask a question, I get buried in another avalanche of options, possibilities, contradictions. I'm afraid that if I keep unraveling, all I'll end up with is enough rope to hang Grant."

"We'll figure it out before it gets to that." Max patted her cheek and got ready to swing out of the car, but Finley stopped him.

"Max, thank you."

"For what, sweetheart?" He straightened in the seat and looked at her as a tear slipped down her cheek. "Fin, talk to me. What's wrong?"

"Nothing and everything. I want to thank you for supporting me in this. I know this isn't what you would have done, but you're working right alongside me to figure it out. Just . . . thanks."

Max leaned over and brushed his lips against hers. "No need. We're in this together, whatever it is. Okay?"

She gave him a smile and returned his kiss. "Let's go."

The two were almost to the front door of the station when the clock tower in the square rang.

"I didn't realize we were that early. We have over thirty minutes before we're due to talk to Grant." Max double-checked his watch.

"You're right. I wasn't paying attention either. Shall we grab a coffee?"

Max inclined his head toward the building across the square. "Instead, let's see if Grant's lawyer is in. Maybe he has some good news."

The attorney was just finishing a sandwich when they walked in.

"A bad habit I learned in the United States. Eating at my desk. My mother considers it barbaric, and my wife just worries about my digestion," the man said, wiping his mouth and dropping the paper napkin in the wastebasket. "I call it a godsend on days like this."

Max and Finley nodded with understanding.

"How may I help you?" the attorney continued. "I am Cosimo Assardi, by the way. But I guess you know that since you came to see me."

"We spoke earlier on the phone. We are friends of Grant Lambert, the man in jail for allegedly murdering his wife," Finley started.

"Ah, yes. You are his ex-wife. He said that you might be stopping in periodically."

Finley smiled. That his ex-wife was there helping him find his current wife didn't seem out of the ordinary to the attorney, if his laid-back manner was any indication.

"Has there been any progress? Have they found the body or a suspected murder weapon? Anything that even says we are dealing with a murder, not just a missing person?" Finley decided to begin to sow the seeds of doubt.

The lawyer dropped back in his chair. "Say that again."

"What? We were just wondering whether the police had found any real evidence against Grant," Finley repeated.

The man rubbed his chin thoughtfully. "Are you an attorney, madam? Because what you just put forth sounds like an argument to raise doubt."

"Does it? Good. That was my intent. I mean, how can they say it's murder without a body or a weapon or anything incriminating? The man just reported his wife missing, and the next thing he knows, he's arrested for her murder. Who says there was even a death?" Finley's voice rose slightly at the last question.

"I see what you are saying, but unfortunately, that is not how the police are looking at it. He can't find his wife, so she must be dead, since they can't find her either. And he must have killed her."

Max shook his head. "There are a lot of jumps in the logic there. Can you help us connect the dots?"

The lawyer laughed. "Not really. I admit, too, that there are gaps, but that is what the police have. Until we come up with something else, he will be tried and likely found guilty."

"How can you convict a man for murder without some evidence that he did it? Any evidence? I haven't heard anything that says he was in any way connected with her disappearance, much less her alleged death." Finley felt the rising level of her frustration and realized she had raised her voice again. She dropped her hands in her lap and hung her head. "I'm sorry."

"No need to be sorry, madam. I understand your anger." The attorney leaned forward. "I will be honest. It does not look good for him right now. But you have given me some other things to raise with the police. Things that will chip away at their case against him so that soon, they will not have—what do you Americans say?—a foot to stand on!"

Finley recognized the saying he was searching for and smiled. "A leg to stand on, but I get your drift. In the meantime, is there anything we can do to help?"

"Find the woman—alive."

Grant was waiting for them in the consultation room, but the excitement he'd had during the morning session had waned. He glanced up only briefly when Finley and Max walked in before returning to stare at the chips in the laminated tabletop.

"I thought you weren't coming," he said resignedly.

"Sorry we're late. We stopped by your attorney's office," Finley shared.

Grant's eyes brightened. "Is there any news? Did they find her? Does it look like I might get out of here?"

"Nothing new, really," Finley whispered.

"But we have another way we're looking at this," Max interjected. "What if she's still alive?"

"That's what I have been saying all along. That I didn't kill her. That she might not even be dead. That she's just missing. That's what I reported." Grant's agitation drew the attention of the guard, who started over to the table before Finley waved him away.

"I don't think we understood fully," Finley explained softly. "We jumped to the conclusion, logically or not, that the police had evidence that she was dead. But in the absence of such evidence—which there's no indication they have—she might indeed be alive."

"We just have to find her," Max added. "And that is where you come in."

"Where do you think she might be?" Finley reached across the table and touched Grant's hand. "Think hard. Where do you think she headed when she left the train?"

Grant shook his head. "I don't know. I have been racking my brain trying to think through scenarios. The logical place—in fact, where I was headed before they arrested me—was Assisi."

"Okay, where else?" Max had pulled out some paper and a pen. "Just give us every possible place to look. Places she mentioned, restaurants she heard about, books she read, things she said she wanted to do, anything."

Grant dropped his head in his hands and ran his fingers through his hair. He sighed deeply. "All I can think about is our argument about Assisi. She was fixated on Assisi."

"Okay. We'll start there. I have a few questions about that. Did she have her purse with her when she left the train?" Finley asked.

"I can't recall. It's all a blur."

Finley sat back. She realized she would have to slow her inquiry if she were to get anything useful from Grant, as despondent as he was. "Did you find her purse in your compartment on the train?"

Grant closed his eyes and shook his head.

Slowly, Finley, slowly. "Do you have any idea how she was going to get to Assisi?"

Grant shook his head again and squeezed his eyes tighter.

"You got off the train in Orvieto under the assumption that she had gotten off in Perugia and headed for Assisi. Is that correct?" Her voice was soft, soothing, almost whispering.

Grant nodded.

"You were going to follow her to Assisi, right?"

Again, he bobbed his head, his eyes still closed.

"By this time, you are off the train. You have both her bag and yours. Are there only two bags, or are there more?"

"Three. There are three. My duffel, hers, and a small backpack we were sharing."

"Okay. Did you check for her passport?"

"Yes, it was in the backpack with mine."

"Good. Did you check for her phone?"

Grant nodded. "I couldn't find it in the pack, so I assumed she took it." He smiled. "She was rarely without her phone."

"Did you try to call her?"

"I did. Several times. When I was on the train and when I got off on the platform in Perugia to look for her. And then again when we were searching the train afterward. I kept calling." Grant's eyes were still closed. He pulled at his hair as the desperation in his voice rose.

Finley observed him as he spoke. *He looked everywhere for her. He was—is—frantic. He loves her.*

"Let's continue, then. You are in Orvieto, heading to Assisi. How are *you* going to get to Assisi?"

"I considered taking the train, but with the schedules, it was going to take too long, so I rented a car."

Finley bolted up straight. *A car.* She had assumed he was traveling solely by train. "So where did you go?"

Grant opened his eyes. "The agent at the car rental desk suggested that I go back through Perugia, but I somehow got lost and ended up in Todi. When I got there, I went to the police station and told them I was looking for my wife. I left a poster."

"You had made posters?" Max looked at Finley. "When?"

"More like flyers, actually. With Blaine's picture and my cell number. I had them made while I was waiting for them to clean the car," Grant said. "There was a little printshop. I figured I needed something to give people, in case they saw her."

"Grant, what were you thinking while you were doing this? What did you think had happened to her?" Finley slowed her words so Grant could fully absorb them.

Grant looked at her vacantly. "I don't really know. All I knew was that she was gone, and I wanted her back."

"Did you think she might be playing a joke on you to get you back for not taking her to Assisi?"

"Initially. And that I wasn't going to fall for it. But then, when I couldn't find her on the train, I got scared."

"Okay. So, by the time you were driving toward Assisi, what were you thinking?"

"It had been hours. That maybe she was sick or hurt. Or maybe she had gotten off and gone to Assisi without me." Grant dropped his head back into his hands. "I don't know."

"Do the police have those flyers?" Max asked.

"I suppose so. They have everything," Grant said.

"How did you end up in a jail here in Spoleto? If they arrested you in Assisi, why not take to you Perugia? It's bigger," Max probed.

"I never made it to Assisi. I kept stopping in small towns and leaving posters. When I got to some little town between here and Spoleto, I stopped and went to leave one. Somehow they got the notion that my wife was dead and that I killed her."

"Did you say or do something that made them suspicious?" Finley asked. "That's a big jump."

"I don't know. I don't know what I said. I was looking pretty bad. I think I had slept in the car, and I might have been rambling. Next thing I knew, I was in the back of a van being transported here." Tears welled up in Grant's eyes. "I didn't do it, Finley. I swear, I didn't do it."

"I believe you, Grant. We just need to find some answers to all the questions that are still hanging there, unanswered."

"We need to find your wife," Max declared. "We're headed to Assisi now. Can we get one of those flyers, do you think?"

"I suppose so. I think I can release all of our belongings, mine and Blaine's, to you. You might find something there that I over-looked," Grant said as they stood to go. "At least you're looking, which is more than I can say for the police. They aren't interested in finding her."

Finley had to agree with Grant's assessment of the situation. The police were convinced Blaine was dead and that Grant had killed her. It was up to Max and Finley to prove otherwise.

On the street, Finley carefully placed the two duffel bags in the trunk of the car before she opened the backpack, looking for the flyers. She found a handful of them shoved into the side pocket. The face of a pretty young woman with a mischievous grin and expressive blue eyes looked up at her.

"Where are you, Blaine? For Grant's sake, tell me where you are," she muttered as she stared back.

6

THE TRIP TO ASSISI HAD yielded nothing besides a delightful late afternoon excursion. The city itself was as charming as Sofia had described with its myriad fountains, castles, and basilicas. Finley and Max could understand why she loved it so much.

A pilgrimage destination for centuries, Assisi was settled by the Umbri, the oldest known inhabitants of Italy, well before the Roman conquest in 295 BC. It had seen its share of rulers, both Italian and foreign, over the centuries. In 2000, the UNESCO declared the church of Saint Francis and surrounding Franciscan structures protected World Heritage sites.

As lovely as their day had been wandering around the city, no one had seen Blaine. Finley and Max walked from the Basilica of Saint Clare to the Temple of Minerva to the Basilica of Saint Francis, showing ticket takers and security guards at all the tourist sights the color flyer of the tiny, blonde American about *this* tall with dimples and deep-blue eyes. But she remained missing, out of sight, lost, even after all their efforts.

Tired and hungry, Finley and Max finally stopped for an afternoon coffee and pastry. They had spent over an hour and a half darting into establishments and stopping random strangers who looked like they might be from the city.

"I was afraid we were going to end up in jail for harassing people," Max complained when they sat down at a café not far from the main square.

"You and me both. People were so nice when they thought we were lost tourists, but they sure didn't want to get involved when they found out we were looking for a missing person."

"Why do you think that is?" Max bit into his *budino di riso*, a thick rice pudding in a pastry shell, getting powdered sugar on his nose.

As Finley leaned over to wipe the offending sugar off Max's face, she stole a bite of pastry as her payment. She chuckled at Max's indignation before responding. "I haven't the slightest. It's not like we were asking for anything other than whether they had seen her."

"I think we were garbed in the Manhattanite invisibility cloak with some of the people we tried to stop," Max remarked, popping the last bite of pastry in his mouth before Finley could claim it.

"The invisibility cloak? What's that?"

"You know, when New Yorkers on the street stare straight ahead and keep walking like you're not there when you try to catch their attention."

"Is it that *we* have an invisibility cloak or that *they* have to maintain their spatial bubble, and since even eyes can pop it, they can't allow eye contact?"

"With New Yorkers, you may have a point, but that shouldn't hold here. All I know is that as soon as the people we approached saw the flyers, their willingness to even look at us vanished."

"Yeah. Beyond frustrating." Finley passed the rest of her pastry over to Max and took a sip of her second espresso, letting the silken crema bathe her tongue.

"So, what do we do now?"

Finley let out a long sigh. "I don't know. I'm completely stumped."

Max gently rubbed the back of her hand with his thumb. "This is our first day—let's get real—our *first time* out looking for her. We can't give up now."

By the time they had returned to the house, Finley and Max had a plan of action. Every day for the rest of the week, they would hit a different small town around Assisi, from Perugia to Spoleto and beyond if necessary. If Blaine had headed toward Assisi, someone would have seen her eventually and call them with information.

As they reached the door of the house, the sweet chords of Ernesto Lecuona's "Malagueña" floated through the air. Max stopped at the threshold and smiled.

"Chuck," he whispered to Finley as he inserted his key and slowly opened the door. "So glad he can still play."

He and Finley stood in the entryway, letting the notes captured by the vaulted ceiling of the vestibule wash over them. When the last note was played, they remained as still as statues until the music's echoes faded.

"I didn't hear you come in," Sofia said as she left the patio, heading for the kitchen, and came upon them standing there. "Come join us. We're starting the cocktail hour off with a bit of music. Chuck felt like playing this afternoon, so I have been treated to a mini-concert."

Taking advantage of the break in the music, Finley greeted Chuck with a kiss on the cheek before drawing back and giving him a deep bow. "I had no idea you played guitar. And I never would have imagined that I knew anyone, ever, who played that well!"

Chuck grinned and pointed at Max. "That boy never told you? Shame on him! He used to take us to weekend gigs all over New Jersey and New York. He would drive and collect the money because me and Jono, the other guy who played with me, would get too drunk to drive ourselves home."

Max laughed at the memory. "I'd pack up the instruments, load them into the car, sit through the session, and then load them back up and collect the money. That's it. Got to listen to some of the best musicians on the East Coast."

"Yeah, we had some nice sessions. Big names sometimes." Chuck leaned the guitar on the stand beside the same elevated barrel chair in which he had sat that morning.

"Would you believe this guy played sessions for Springsteen and Aretha Franklin?" Max said. "He was all over the place in terms of genre. They didn't care. They just wanted the best."

"Put me through grad school—"

"And paid for the down payment on our first apartment!" Sofia added.

"And now, I'm back to playing rhythm guitar and getting excited if I can get all the way through 'Malagueña' without losing control." Chuck stared at his hands and shook his head ruefully.

Finley put her hand on his shoulder. "I know it's disappointing, but if it eases the pain any, remember that, even at your worst, you play better than most at their best."

"You're right, but it still saddens me." Chuck gave her a soulful smile. "I'm luckier than most with ALS, I suppose. Mine is starting from the feet up. I know it will hit my hands at some point, but until then, I play what I can."

"Do you mind if I record some of your sessions?" Max asked, taking the glass of Chiani Sofia passed him.

"Record them?" Chuck chortled. "You don't want save any of this drivel!"

"You should, Chuck," Sofia said. "You've done some interesting arrangements of old standards in order to work around some of the fingering challenges you've had."

Chuck picked up his guitar and silently played with some of the fingering before laying the instrument across his lap. "Maybe. We'll see. In the meantime, tell me what you found out this afternoon."

Finley glanced at Max. As determined as she had been to find some sign that Blaine was alive, she was resigned to the fact that uncovering that evidence wouldn't be easy. "Not much, but we're going to stick with it. My gut says she's done a bunk, as the Brits say, and is out there somewhere."

"We just hit Assisi and a couple of other nearby places today, but we've mapped out some other towns between here and Perugia that she might have traveled to," Max added.

"What do you think is her objective if she is still alive? I mean, why hasn't she called her husband to let him know she is not dead?" Sofia wondered aloud. She placed a large platter with antipasti in front of Max and smiled. "This will hold you over until we fix dinner."

"She may not know that anyone's looking for her." Finley picked up a piece of a soft Italian cheese and wrapped it in a thin slice of air-dried meat. "Remember that, according to Grant, they had had a big blowout over going to Assisi. She might want to make him stew."

"This long? I mean, it's been what? Four or five days?" Max looked incredulous.

"Maybe she's waiting for him to make the first move," Finley countered.

Max turned to look at his partner. "Would you leave me in the dark that long?"

"It depends. If I was always the one who gave in, I might be spiteful enough to refuse to capitulate this time."

Max opened his mouth to speak but closed it and adopted a look that was somewhere between puzzled and hurt. In response, Chuck burst out laughing. "That boy doesn't know what to think now. Girl, you've got him confused! Speak, boy. Say something."

"Chuck, leave the man alone. He hadn't anticipated her response. Give him space to think," Sofia said.

Max tried again. He drew in a breath to speak and just as quickly let it out again. On the third try, he spoke, his voice soft and still bewildered. "Fin, if we had had a row like that and you had stormed off, what would you have wanted me to do?"

"What would you have naturally done?" Finley asked, turning on the bench to look at him.

"I don't know. I know now that whatever it was, it would likely have been the wrong thing."

"You don't know that." Finley fixed her eyes on her husband's. Their time in Morocco came to mind. "I suspect that if I had left in a huff, you, like Grant, would have assumed I was making my own way to Assisi, and you would have sent me a message saying you were sorry and you would meet me there."

"I would."

"And that would be the end of it."

"It would."

"But that's not what happened here," Chuck interjected.

"Because it couldn't," Finley explained. "Grant was trying to follow that course of action but got arrested. So now, we have to think about what Blaine's next logical step would be if she didn't hear from her husband."

"Call her mother," Sofia mumbled under her breath, almost so softly that Finley missed it.

Finley redirected her gaze from Max to Sofia. "You are brilliant! Yes, she would have called her mother."

She bounded off the bench and started to pace. "Yes, she would have called her mother," she repeated, staring out over the verdant countryside.

"But we don't know her mother, so we can't ask her," Max reminded Finley.

"True, but we can ask Grant tomorrow whether he asked his in-laws if Blaine had called. They got him the lawyer, remember? So they have communicated."

"Surely, they would have said something. Those are heartless people if they know their son-in-law is sitting in jail for their daughter's murder, and they haven't let on that she is alive," Sofia muttered, shaking her head.

Finley stopped midstride. "You're right. You are so right." She dropped back down onto the bench. "That shoots that angle down. So we're back to square one. She has to be dead. Even if she was mad at Grant, she wouldn't let her parents suffer. And if she called them, they wouldn't let him be tried for a murder that didn't happen."

The group was silent for several moments as the reality of Finley's logic sunk in. As much as she had wanted to believe that Amata's supposition was a possibility, the sequence she had just gone through had led her back to the inconvertible truth that Blaine was most likely dead.

"We can still leave flyers in the towns we didn't hit today," Max said quietly, sliding over to give Finley a hug. "Nothing ventured, nothing gained."

Sometime during the evening interlude, when Chuck took another break from his mixed set of Isaac Albéniz, John Mayer, and the Gipsy Kings, Finley headed upstairs for a shawl. The evening air had acquired a nip that Sofia said foretold a later shower. As she passed the other guest bedroom on her way to grab another blanket for the bed from linen closet at the end of the hall, she thought she heard a bell. Standing in the doorway, she leaned in and listened for it again but was greeted with silence.

It was only on the return trip, when she heard a faint ringing sound, that she entered the room and stood, waiting for another ring. When it came, she followed the sound to one of the duffel bags Grant had asked her to store for him. She opened the bag and dug deep into its side, feeling around for what might be shaped like a phone. The bag she knew from the contents was Blaine's, but how had her phone come to be there? Grant had said she had taken it.

The phone rang several times before it stopped. Even so, Finley continued to rummage in the bag until she found Blaine's iPhone. The screen was still lit, allowing Finley to bring the latest call information back into view.

There was a conversation thread from the last number that had started several months earlier. Finley was ready to move on, suspecting it was not relevant to finding Blaine, until she saw the latest series of entries.

fyeo did u make the jump

Several minutes later, presumably when Blaine failed to answer, the texter sent another message.

Whr r u? Wnt to pla agreed bt u not thr. pcm

Another few minutes passed before there was a missed call and then the final message.

CM. LMK WH U R.

The last call, the one that Finley had missed, was just six hours after the last text message.

Finley hit the screen again to keep the phone from closing.

"Max!" she called as she headed down the stairs, her shawl flowing behind her. "Max!"

Max met her at the bottom of the stairs and drew her into a tight embrace when she reached him. "What's the matter? You scared of the dark?"

Finley shook her head and then held up the phone to show him the screen. "No, silly. But take a look at this."

She turned the screen toward him and scrolled through the conversation thread. "What do you make of that?"

"Hard to tell." Max took the phone from Finley and looked at the texts again. "Whose phone is this?"

"Blaine's."

"How did you get Blaine's phone?"

"It was in one of the duffel bags Grant gave us. Don't ask me how the phone got there. Now we have a fairly recent series of messages that suggest Amata may have been right. Blaine isn't dead."

Max shook his head and chuckled. "You're going to give me whiplash, woman. Before dinner, you said there was no way she could be alive. And now you say this says she *is* alive. Which is it?"

"I don't know. All I know is that this phone needs to be handed over to the police, and the messages need to be followed up on. This may be Grant's get-out-of-jail ticket."

By the time Max and Finley got to the police station, it was just after 10:00 p.m. The streets were empty except for a few barking dogs that disrupted the quiet of the night. The rain hadn't started, but the air was heavy in anticipation. At the station, Finley let Max do the talking. She focused on touching the screen periodically so that she didn't have to enter a password.

"How may I help you?" the night duty officer asked in Italian.

Max explained that they may have new evidence in Grant's case that suggested his wife was still alive. His Italian might not have been fluent, but it was proficient enough to convey the importance of the information they had found.

To say the officer's reaction was underwhelming would have been an understatement. The man raised his eyes to look at Blaine's phone before lowering them barely a second later to return to his reading of a newspaper open on the desk in front of him.

"I'm not sure you understand the importance of what we found on this phone. This may very well clear the man of all suspicion," Max emphasized.

The officer nodded without raising his eyes. He stuck out his hand and waited. "Please leave the phone with me. I will see that it gets to the officer in charge. If he has any questions, I am sure he will call you."

When Max drew his breath in preparation for the barrage of invectives he was readying for launch, Finley touched his arm and signaled the need for a strategic pause in the action.

"It's not worth it to lose you temper. We have pictures of everything in the thread," she whispered. "Give him the phone, and we'll take the screenshots to Mr. Assardi in the morning, or the other attorney in his office if he's not in."

Max flared his nostrils and pursed his lips for a full minute before relaxing his shoulders. "Let's get this guy's name before we leave the phone with him and ask for a receipt for it before we just hand it over. The nerve."

Finley made sure that Max was back in the car before she allowed him to vent his frustration fully. "They're determined to have Grant thrown in jail and the key buried whether he's guilty or not. Whether there has even been a murder or not! I have never seen anything like this!"

"And I hope to goodness you never do again, but the only way we can help Grant is to stay out of jail ourselves." Finley laid her hand on his. "We have to find her, dead or alive!"

7

MAX HAD CALMED DOWN BY the time he and Finley arrived at Assardi's office the following morning. They were in luck; the attorney was in and greeted them warmly.

"I am profoundly sorry for the police reaction you received last night," Assardi said when Max recounted their attempt to deliver Blaine's phone to the police the previous evening. "They aren't used to the involvement of concerned citizens. Most people stay as far away from the police station as they can."

"I understand, but when a man's life is on the line, I guess I expected more of a sense of urgency," Finley said, taking a large gulp of the espresso the man had served them.

"You say you have pictures of the texts that were sent?" the attorney asked.

Max nodded. "We were afraid we would eventually be blocked from using the phone without the password, so Finley took a few pictures of the screen."

"I'll send them to you now." Finley opened her phone and scrolled to the frames she had shot of the text messages.

Assardi pulled up the messages when his phone pinged. His mouth quirked as he read, his gaze intense. He looked up and muttered to no one in particular, "She is alive."

"That is what it seems. Now, to find her," Max said.

"Do you think she is hiding?" the lawyer wondered, his eyes focused on a point outside the window of his office building.

"From whom? And why? And who sent these messages?" Finley leaned into the questions. "That's the part that doesn't make sense. If she wanted out of the marriage, just ask for a divorce. If someone else is after her, why not let Grant know so he can help?"

"But Grant said everything was fine. They were having a second honeymoon. No indication of any problems or concerns." Max tilted his head in confusion.

"That's what he says. But maybe she saw it differently. We have only one side of the story," Finley offered. "Maybe she wanted out but didn't know how to end it. Or maybe she didn't tell him she was in trouble."

"Faking your death and leaving your husband with a life sentence in a foreign jail? That's pretty cold, even if you were scared of something," Max said.

"In any event, this at least raises some doubt. Maybe it will slow down a fast conviction." Assardi reread the texts. "Any idea who the person sending the messages is?"

"No, but we are headed over to the jail to talk to Grant now. Perhaps he will know."

However, the opportunity to raise the question with Grant never presented itself. When Finley and Max arrived at the police station, Grant already had guests.

A tall, patrician, middle-aged man and a stylishly coiffed woman in a perfectly fitted pale-blue Escada pantsuit were just taking their places at the table where Grant sat. The woman checked the bottom of the seat with slightly veiled disgust before lowering herself onto the chair. Grant jumped up as Finley and Max walked in and stood awkwardly beside his guests.

"Beth, Howard, let me introduce Finley Blake and her husband, Max," Grant mumbled by way of a hasty introduction. "Finley, Max, these are Blaine's parents."

Finley could feel Grant's discomfort even before he spoke. She refused the chair Grant offered in an effort to defuse the tension, signaling her intention to leave soon.

"We just stopped by to see how you were doing. We didn't realize you had guests." Finley smiled politely at Grant's in-laws. The set of Blaine's mother's mouth told Finley all she needed to know about how his mother-in-law felt about her presence.

"That was so kind of you to assist Grant in this awful situation," the woman started, her voice a monotonous Locust Valley drone.

"We were glad to be able to help. When did you arrive?" Finley shifted to more directly engage the woman as her husband appeared to run his eyes carefully over Finley, then Max.

Is he inspecting us? For what? Suitability to talk to his son-in-law? Wonder if we'll pass inspection. Finley's lips quirked upward into a half smile that must have looked like a smirk because the man quickly dropped his eyes when their eyes met.

"This morning. We came directly from the airport to see Grant," the woman intoned.

Finley nodded. "Yes, of course. Well, we won't distract you any further." She shifted her gaze to Grant, who sat uncomfortably, staring at his folded hands. "Grant, let us know if you need anything." He jumped slightly when he realized the comment was addressed to him.

Before he could respond, the woman interjected. "I think we have everything well in hand. Again, thank you, but we'll take it from here."

With that, Finley and Max were dismissed. They nodded a goodbye to Grant and then his in-laws before retreating out the door, past the sergeant's desk to the street below.

For the first thirty seconds, neither of them said a word. Stopped on the cobbled sidewalk in front of the station, they stood,

Finley with her mouth pursed into a tight bud, Max with his eyes fixed on Finley. After a few moments, Finley struck off, striding purposefully up the street.

"Where're you going?" Max struggled to keep up.

"I need a drink."

"Fin, it's only eleven o'clock! Are you sure want a drink, not coffee?"

"I'll have a drink, thank you very much."

Max did not answer. Instead, he drew alongside and took her hand in his as they continued to the go-to café they had found a few days ago tucked behind the main square.

"That woman is insufferable!" Finley had held her tongue until they were seated and had ordered—a white wine for her, and for Max, a cappuccino and *sfogliatella riccia*, a flaky custard-filled pastry.

The owner, who also served as a waiter during the morning hours, looked at Max with a raised brow when Finley ordered her wine but said nothing. Max gave him a sad smile in response.

Finley muttered again, mainly to herself, "She should have been the one pushed from a train, not Blaine."

"Well, we now suspect that Blaine wasn't pushed but jumped from the train, if that text is to be believed." Max took a bite of the pastry that had just been placed before him.

"That's what we have to focus on—finding Blaine and her accomplice!"

"They didn't mention it, but don't you think her parents have already hired someone to find her?"

"Possibly, since we know the police aren't looking for her." Finley stared absentmindedly at the people passing along the narrow street. A well-dressed man in his forties caught her eye. "But what would they be looking for—a person or a body?"

"I'm sure her parents are hoping to find her alive. I can't believe they would be so dismissive of her—or so solicitous of Grant—if they thought she was dead."

"If they are assuming she's still alive, then what is their explanation for why she left in the first place?" Finley turned to look at Max quizzically.

"You raise a good point. If she's alive, they must figure she has a good reason for not contacting anyone."

"Do you think she has a history of running off? That's why her mother is throwing up the defenses?"

"That would make more sense than anything else I can think of."

"I mean, if they thought she had amnesia or was taken ill or something, they would have asked us to look for her as well as anyone else they, or we, knew." Finley looked at Max over the rim of her wineglass. "And they would have been arguing with the police for more people to search for her. There would have been some sense of urgency."

Max nodded his head vigorously, tapping the table to punctuate his thoughts. "That's what was missing for me back there— urgency! None of those three acted like this was a big deal, like there was a rush to find her. Dead or alive."

"Quite honestly, we have been putting more energy in this than I suspect they will."

"You're probably right."

"But I wonder *why?*" Finley drew out the last word.

Max watched her, deep in thought, and waited.

When Finley turned to look at Max, her eyes had pooled with tears.

"Sweetheart, what's wrong?" Max asked, his brow knitted with concern.

"She didn't call her mother. With a mother like that, she wouldn't have. Do you think they have written her off as dead?" Finley whispered.

Max took a breath before answering. "Perhaps. The Goddards remind me a lot of my parents. New England reserve on steroids. They probably believe she's indeed dead at someone else's hand.

A private investigator will take care of finding the real killer and returning her body. They will focus on getting Grant out of jail and back to his children in the United States. If they pay enough, their hope is that this ugly business will be over by the end of the week."

"That's sad." Finley sighed, wiping the tear that had escaped and was running down her cheek. "I would hate to think that Mama and Daddy, and you, wouldn't be frantically looking for me if I dropped off the face of the earth like that."

Max took her hand and kissed the inside of her wrist. "You know we would. We'd search to the end of the universe and back for you. However long it took."

"I feel for those children," Finley said resignedly.

Max chuckled softly. "Well, I survived. Not all families are as loving as yours. But even as distant as mine was, I was blessed to have found someone as kindhearted as you. Those kids will too. In the meantime, we need to get on with our lives."

"You're right. Grant has his in-laws now. He doesn't need us." Finley gulped down the last of her wine and put money down for their drinks. "Let's go to the market. Sofia needed lemons and a few other things."

"Shall we try the one at Campello sul Clitunno? Chuck said the town is quite a scenic little place known for its olive oil production. And we need to get away from here."

The open-air market in Campello sul Clitunno was still in full swing when Finley and Max parked the car near the water and headed toward the center of town. A massive park with swans and ducks occupied both banks of the river that ran through the town. Arched stone bridges connected the shores as weeping willows dipped their branches into the pristine water.

Chuck had explained that the small towns clustered around Spoleto rotated the market days so that farmers could offer fresh products throughout the week without undercutting one another's prices. The market days were set so that customers knew where to go on which day. Today was Campello's day, and the market was bustling.

Finley passed a basket to Max and slung another one over her arm as they made their way along the rows of tables heaped with carrots and greens, early summer fruits and herbs, wines, cheeses, and olive oils. Finley had just finished paying for a handful of large, fragrant, local lemons when she heard her name. Turning toward the sound, she caught sight of Mario and Elena Fuscati, Sofia and Chuck's truffle farmer friends, at a pop-up stall displaying truffle oil and butter as well as a pecorino with a vein of black truffles.

"What a pleasant surprise! Come to experience our local market, I see." Elena, radiant as always in a floral-patterned peasant blouse with a scooped neck, stood to greet her, pecking her once on each cheek before embracing Max. Max and Mario shook hands and clapped each other on the back.

"Yes. Sofia wanted a few things, so we figured we'd pick them up here in town rather than in the supermarket off the motorway. A lot more fun, and we know it's fresh," Finley said.

"Do you stick to one market with your stall, or do you move around to different towns?" Max asked the couple as Finley surveyed the different products on offer.

"We tend to rotate," Mario replied. "Unless we are truffling. Then we are more selective about the markets we attend."

"We're retired, so we get to pick and choose what we want to do on any given day." Elena chuckled.

Finley, having decided on cheese instead of truffle butter, picked up a piece of pecorino and signaled to Max to pay.

"No, no. That is on the house, as you Americans say," Elena said, shaking her head. "We want you to experience all of Umbria as our friends."

Mario piped in. "To that point, why don't you join us this afternoon? We are going to go truffle hunting."

"Isn't it early in the season?" Max asked.

"Yes, but one of the dogs found a few that were ripe, so they may have come in early. We were going to take a walk through the woods to see," Mario replied.

"In the worst case, you get a nice walk in the country. You see our farm—" Elena said.

"And you get a good glass of wine at the end for your troubles!" Mario added.

Finley turned to Max hopefully. "We could still be back in time to have a late dinner with Sofia and Chuck."

"Of course. We won't keep you all night," Elena reassured them.

"I wish Chuck could still walk the paths. Only last year, he was out with the dogs." Mario shook his head sadly.

"It is tragic, but he seems to be managing it well. He was playing for us last night, which was amazing," Max said before smiling at an expectant Finley. "To your invitation, we accept. What time? Where?"

"And what do we need to wear?" Finley looked down at her springlike dress and knew this attire wasn't appropriate.

Elena laughed. "Yes, you will have to go change, but pants, a shirt, and trainers will be fine."

"We'll probably head out about sixteen thirty or seventeen hundred. We aren't far from where you are. I'll send a locator." Mario had already pulled out his phone and was sending the information to Max and Finley.

The foursome said their farewells, and then Finley and Max searched the rest of the tables for the other items on their grocery list. With two baskets filled with jams, salamis, cheeses, fruits, vegetables, and bread, the two headed back to the car and started off toward Chuck and Sofia's.

Max took the longer way back to the house, winding through tiny villages that he would have had a hard time finding on the map. Both he and Finley were silent, transfixed by the idyllic rolling hills spotted with herds of grazing sheep interspersed between the ancient clusters of houses and buildings that made up some of the villages along the route.

Having skipped lunch to do the shopping, and with only coffee, a roll, and wine for breakfast, Finley was starting to feel peckish. Even from the back, the fragrance of the peaches and strawberries they had just bought was distractingly heady.

"I'm going to have to dip into the provisions we just got. I think we have enough bread and fruit that we can have a bit without Sofia being too short on supplies. My stomach is growling. Can I get you some bread or a peach?"

Max chuckled. "We do have a car. We can always go for more fruit or bread tomorrow morning. Especially since we don't have to head to the jail anymore."

"That's true. Peach or strawberries?" Finley turned in her seat and reached into the back to pull off a butt of bread before passing it to Max.

"Why don't you feed me strawberries like they do in the movies?" Max joked, casting Finley a sly smile. "I'll be very careful that I don't run off the road!"

She laughed. She had just reached for a peach for herself and some strawberries for Max when they entered one of the smaller villages. A couple standing off the road caught her eye. The woman was petite, dressed in jeans and a button-down shirt, a straw hat pulled over the blonde hair that framed her face. The man was dark-haired, tall, and tanned. He leaned down and kissed her as she left the narrow sidewalk and stood at the mouth of one of the small streets that splintered off the main road.

For a moment, Finley froze. *It can't be her. But what if it is? Don't take the chance.* Quickly recovering, she pulled her hand out of the basket and began rummaging around the back seat for her satchel.

"Fin, you okay?" Max slowed the car and glanced at her as Finley grabbed her camera and rolled down the back window. Max had almost stopped the car, trying to figure out what had attracted her concentrated attention.

Finley, glad that the car was now moving at a crawl, rested her lens on the back of the seat and started shooting. *Something from this has to come out. This is our only chance. It's her. It has to be her. But who is the man?*

The man and woman, oblivious to anyone around them, deepened the embrace. The prolonged kiss allowed Finley to zoom in and capture several shots that more clearly showed the woman's face. After several moments, the couple parted, talking briefly before the woman walked up one of the side streets.

Finley continued pressing the shutter, recording the scene as Max crept the car along the narrow main road. When a truck behind Max's vehicle honked, Max sped up and pulled over onto the pitted sidewalk. Her view partially blocked by a crumbling colonnade, Finley just managed to freeze the parting frames of the man looking up and down the road before he followed the blonde woman up the cobbled street.

8

FINLEY WAS OUT OF THE car and down the road before Max could even turn off the ignition. She wandered up the narrow, cobbled street where she had seen the couple turn. From this vein of a street, other capillary alleyways flowed into what looked like old stone houses and multifamily dwellings. She could hear the voices of children and families through the open windows and smell the redolence of onions, garlic, and oil that signaled the beginning preparations for the evening meal, but she saw no one in the doorways or side streets. Finley turned around and met Max at the top of the street.

"Who did you see that had you hurrying off like that?"

"Blaine! I thought I saw Blaine with a man," Finley explained, pulling up a few frames as proof. "There—what do you think?"

In some pictures, the angle of the shot or the woman's hat prevented seeing anything more than her blonde hair. The last frames of the man, however, were better. For those, the fact that the car had been stopped and the man's face had not been obscured by them kissing allowed ready recognition of her companion.

"Hard to tell, but that may be her. The hair matches. And the size." Max scrolled back and forth between the photos. "Pity you can't see under the hat to get a better glimpse of her face."

"I wish I could have switched to a telephoto. But there was no time."

Max kissed her forehead. "You did very well under the circumstances."

"What do we do now?"

Max scanned the street. "Not many people around, but we can put up a few flyers and see what crawls out of the woodwork."

"Good idea. If nothing else, it will let her know that the gig is up. Whatever she was trying to do by disappearing didn't work. There are people looking for her."

They walked the short main road, posting flyers in the bank, the post office, and one of the small grocery stores. Finley started back toward the car while Max finished a conversation about the missing woman with a clothing store owner off the main street. When Finley reached the mouth of the cobbled street, she all but ran into the man she had seen earlier.

"So sorry," Finley said as she stepped back to confirm it was the same man. He was taller up close than he had appeared at first glance, with an open, engaging smile.

"*Scusi!*" The man also retreated a step, his hands in the air as he avoided a collision.

As he did, he cast a glance at the flyer with Blaine's picture in Finley's hand. In an instant, the smile melted, and the color drained from his face. He raced for a car parked in front of a small shopping arcade.

Finley seized on the change in his demeanor and followed him closely, pointing to the flyer. "Do you recognize this woman? Do you know her?"

The man opened the car door quickly and jumped in, muttering in Italian as he sped off down the road. "*Non capisco. Parlo solo italiano.*"

Max, hearing the squeal of tires, rushed to Finley's side. "What was that about? Are you okay?"

Finley nodded as she checked her last frame. She smiled. "His license plate number."

"Who is he? What did he say?"

"Not much of anything besides that he spoke only Italian. But he recognized her picture. He almost fainted when he saw it. That's the man in the earlier shots. Now to find out who he is!"

Max took Finley in his arms. "Good work, sweetheart, but you scared me to death. All I heard was you screaming at him and then the sound of his tires peeling off. I thought I would find you splayed in the middle of the road when I came around the corner."

"Was I screaming?" Finley looked up at him. "I'm sorry. I didn't realize it. The people in the houses must think I'm mad."

Max kissed her nose. "Mad as a hatter—and sly as a fox. Now we'd better go, or we'll miss our truffle hunt. We can contact the police later. As if they'll care."

Back at the house, Max shared some of the events of their day with Chuck and Sofia while Finley ran upstairs to get changed. Sofia and Chuck were delighted that Mario and Elena had invited them for an impromptu truffle hunt.

"If the summer ones are coming in early, we can take a walk around our woods tomorrow and see if we have any ripe ones," Chuck said, taking a sip of a new Sangiovese. "We generally are a couple of weeks behind the rest of the farms, but who knows?"

"Can you ask Mario if we can borrow his dogs tomorrow or later this week?" Sofia poured two small glasses of Chianti and held them out for Max and Finley. "We gave up the dogs last year, but Chuck can still take his chair on the boardwalk we built between the trees. You'll see."

Finley had just come down, having changed into her jeans, a chambray shirt, and a pair of black Ariats. She had wrapped a long, sheer khaki-colored scarf twice around her neck.

"Thanks," Finley said as she accepted the glass of wine and took a seat on the bench across from Chuck. "Did Max tell you about our adventure this afternoon?"

"No, I was just getting to that part. Why don't you tell them?" Max took a piece of bread and salami and leaned back.

"We think we saw Blaine! Maybe it was wishful thinking, but the woman we saw was the same size and her hair was the same color as the picture of Blaine that Grant gave us."

"Where was this that you saw her?" Sofia had claimed a seat on the bench beside Finley.

"We took the long way back from Spoleto and went to Campello sul Clitunno market for groceries. It was one of those little villages between there and here. I didn't even look at the name," Max explained.

"There was a bank and a post office. And a really cute dress shop up one of the side streets," Finley added.

"Did it have a square?" Chuck asked.

"No, just a narrow main road and these little arched arcades with a few alleyways and parking spaces off that. A couple of the little arcades had fountains at the entry. That was it."

"I think that is San Giacomo. I know where you were." Chuck nodded. "I'll show you on a more detailed map. That'll help the police find it."

"So you found her!" Sofia patted Finley's knee. "Now to go get her and make her admit that she is not dead, so Grant can go free."

"Then he can divorce her!" Chuck muttered. "I don't think that man is going to want to stay married to a woman who does these sorts of high jinks!"

"Have you gone to the police yet?" Sofia asked.

Finley shook her head. "I need to see if I can get any of the pictures clear enough to see her face. With what we have, they'd show us the door. The man can be seen, but not her."

"And she got his license plate number when he sped off," Max added. "They should be able to find him. If they find him, they'll hopefully find her."

"Sounds like you had a productive day," Chuck remarked. "Now, you better hightail it over to Mario's and grab yourselves a few truffles!"

When Max pulled into the tree-lined lane that led to the Fuscatis' farm, he and Finley thought they would see the house in short order. However, it was almost five minutes before the tiled roof peeked through the trees. On the drive to the house, the landscape alternated between clusters of light-dappled woods and expanses of spring-green fields. The road, little more than a goat path, bisected the property, splitting the woods, fields, and hills equally on both sides.

The house burst from the last outcropping of trees like a surprise package, bright and airy, multitiered, and wrapped in flowering vines and lattice. An elegant yet vibrant ochre color, it nestled into the undulating olive-green hills comfortably, like a jewel in a velvet case.

"I thought Chuck and Sofia's house was gorgeous, but this is over-the-top. Who do you think has the money?" Finley leaned forward to catch the full grandeur of the house through the windshield before getting out.

"Aren't you a catty one?" Max laughed as he slid out of the car.

"As if you weren't wondering the same!" Finley countered under her breath just as Elena came up the path.

"We are around back, packing the cart," she said, waving them toward her.

At the back of the house on the lower green, Mario and another man sporting a green quilted vest, dark-gray pants, and a slate bibbed hat were loading baskets and what looked like a cooler onto a horse cart. A small bay horse waited patiently for the men to finish.

"Welcome to the farm. I hope you didn't have any trouble finding it," Mario said as he gave final instructions to the other man.

Max shook his head. "No, the pin led us right here. And, of course, Chuck had given us all the landmarks to look out for."

"We have a few more hours of sunlight, and then the moon will light our way," Elena said. "Matteo and Nico will join us to handle the dogs. We'll see what we find."

"Before we forget, Chuck and Sofia asked if they could borrow the dogs tomorrow or sometime later in the week. Chuck wants to see if any of his truffles are ripe," Finley said.

"Of course. I will let the handlers know. Chuck likes working with Bosco, one of the Labrador mixes. And we'll find another one to join him," Mario responded, picking up walking sticks and handing them to the others. "Let's go."

The group set off down the center path that continued past the house and into another woods hugging the base of a nearby hill. The horse cart had departed along an adjacent road that was slightly wider but was still made only of pressed dirt. The fallow fields they passed were flecked with white and yellow meadow flowers. Along the fence line and intermittently in clumps off the path, wild rosemary grew, scenting the air with its aromatic fragrance.

"So how often do you go hunting in a season?" Finley walked with Elena and one of the dogs, a poodle-looking Lagotto Romagnolo, who disregarded the handler's presence and attached herself to Elena's side. Max, Mario, and the handlers hiked ahead.

Periodically, Elena would reach down and ruffle the dog's ear, prompting her to rub her head against Elena's leg. "Bella is still in training. I should discipline her and send her back to Nico, but she is such a sweet girl that I spoil her. I will pay the price later when she has to be retrained as a truffler, but she is young."

Elena went on, "We walk almost every day around the property, but we don't always take the dogs. And you can't hunt truffles without the dogs for environmental reasons."

"Why is that?"

"To find the truffles, since they are underground, you would have to dig little holes all over the woods. The human nose can't detect them. What a mess that would be."

"Once the dogs find them, what happens?" Finley had visions of the dogs retrieving truffles like they would a ball.

"The handlers will take the dogs to the best areas, which are well-kept secrets, sometimes passed down from generation to generation."

"How long has this property been in the family?"

"The Fuscati family has owned this land since the sixteenth century. Someone from the family has been hunting truffles on this land since then."

Finley paused to take in the magnitude of that historical tradition. "What happens if a line doesn't have children?"

"Then a cousin or distant relative comes and takes over. It is like the English and their entailments, I suppose," Elena laughed and then inclined her head toward Mario and the handlers. "They are taking us to a very rich area. We should be lucky."

"How many do you expect to find today?"

"It will be a fairly short hunt today, so maybe a handful or so." Elena gave Finley a side-glance. "Mainly so we can eat and drink!"

"Well, this is a real treat for us. Max has been eating the truffles at Sofia's like they are M&M's. I think he has run through a few thousand dollars' worth, mixing them in his eggs, his pasta, and his *pasta e fagioli*. Last night, Sofia made him a grilled cheese with pecorino and truffles! He's gotten spoiled."

"Tonight, we will make him work for his supper. He can bring back his finds to Sofia."

The dogs had entered a wooded area slightly off the path and, at the handlers' command, began to sniff the ground at the base of some of the trees. Bella, anxious to join in the fun, ran to Nico, waiting for his command. When he sent her off, she wandered the undergrowth, her nose to the ground. It took only a few minutes before she started pawing the earth. After she had moved some of the soil back, Nico called her off and passed the spade to Elena.

"No, Bella found this one for you," Elena said, handing the tool to Finley.

"What am I supposed to do now?" Finley asked, taking the tool like it was a loaded gun.

Nico bent down to show her what Bella had found. "This one is close to the surface, so you can actually get it with your hand— but gently. They look rugged and ugly, but they are quite *delicato*."

Finley followed Nico's lead and leaned down until she could see what looked like a dirty, withered, brownish, desiccated tangerine. She took her hand and gently brushed back the dirt to unearth it.

"A very big one. I am surprised at the size so early." Elena took the truffle in her hand and then held it to her nose. "Smell that. I bet this one will have nice marbling. That is what you want."

Elsewhere around the woods, the handlers were following the dogs, watching that they didn't dig too deep or too hard and damage the precious tubers. Bella was on a roll, finding four in quick succession. Each time, she came back to Elena for a pat and verbal praise.

"Do we have enough to justify some wine?" Mario called out after a while.

Elena and Finley gave him the thumbs-up, and the group headed down a path that led out of the woods toward a field that edged the forest.

"This part of the woods used to have tenant farmers on it until fifty or so years ago. Then all the young people stopped farming, and the old farmers died off. You'll see old cottages among the trees. It can get spooky at night," Elena shared as she pointed to the remains of what used to be a tenant's house.

When they reached the clearing, the horse cart had been laid out with a tablecloth, wine carafes, and glasses, as well as an antipasto that included a range of cheeses and salamis, pastramis, and pickled vegetables. A round of freshly made bread with pots of honey, fig jam, and olive oil complemented the spread.

"You have worked hard for your wine. Now, your reward!" Mario ceremoniously presented Finley with the first glass of Chianti, the syrupy, chocolate-berry smell wafting up from the bowl of the glass. Her first sip evoked an elixir of the gods. She closed her eyes in response and sighed.

"That is the reaction I want from my wines!" Mario gazed at her proudly. "Pure enchantment!"

Finley blushed. "I didn't realized I had sighed so loudly. This is sublime! I didn't know you made wine as well as farmed truffles."

"We're Italian. Every household around here makes wine, normally Chianti or Sangiovese. Only certain families sell it. We just make it for ourselves—and our friends," Elena explained.

"Elena's family made wine in this region during the time of the Romans!"

"Mario, you exaggerate! But my family has been making wine for centuries."

"That is the only reason my mama let her into the family! She came from good traditions."

Elena playfully punched her husband's arm and raised her glass. "To new friends and old traditions!"

They had just lowered their glasses when one of the dogs let out a mournful howl. Matteo and Nico, who had been leaning against the side of the cart, eating bread and cheese, looked around to account for the dogs.

"Bella!" they shouted at once and strode off toward the sound of the howls. The other dogs dashed off in pursuit.

"What in goodness's name is happening?" Mario put down his glass and tromped off in the direction of the noise. The others followed.

By the time they reached the area where the dogs had stopped, all three dogs had joined in the baying and howling, pacing wildly around the base of what looked like an old well. The handlers tried to call them off, but seconds after they quieted, they resumed barking and howling.

"That well has been closed over for years. What are you crying about?" Mario snapped at the dogs testily. "Quiet! Quiet now!"

"Mario, maybe something fell in somehow. A puppy or another animal. They are trying to tell us something. At least check to see," Elena insisted.

Mario conceded after a few minutes and signaled to the men to remove the well cover and check. As the men approached, it was clear that the cover had been moved recently. It sat back off the well lip, exposing over half of the well opening.

"Good gracious. Let's pray it is not a child. There are breaks in the fences at intervals, and the village children like to explore," Elena said solemnly, holding her breath as the men slid the cover off and dropped it to the ground.

None of the men from the farm were too anxious to peer into the well's abyss to see what had the dogs in such a lather. While the dogs continued howling, the men stood silently, debating who would take the first look. Tired of the dithering, Mario impatiently pulled a flashlight from his pocket and approached the edge. He shone the beam deep into the well and peered inside. Something caught the light. He gasped and jumped back in terror, almost dropping the flashlight.

"*Santa Maria! Un corpo. C'è un corpo. È morta. Holy Mother, pray for her. She's dead!*"

9

MAX PRIED THE FLASHLIGHT FROM Mario's fingers and approached the well lip. Expecting to hear the gurgling water of a naturally fed spring well, he was surprised to be met by silence. He flicked the torch on and held it over the edge. He was not shocked by what he saw. Given Mario's description, he knew before he saw her that it was Blaine whose body lay at the bottom of the dry well.

"It's Blaine," he said softly.

Finley gulped. "But how? We just saw her. She was alive a few hours ago."

She reached for the flashlight to see for herself. Instead, Max stepped back, pointing the shaft of light so Finley could see the body sprawled in the mud at the base of the well. The dead woman wore the same jeans and shirt that Finley had seen her in earlier in the afternoon. Sadness, remorse, and fear twisted Finley's innards. She closed her eyes and moved away from the edge of the well. Max took her elbow to steady her as she turned to walk away.

"Why? Why would anyone kill her?" Finley searched Max's face for answers.

"I don't know, sweetheart. We need to call the police," Max stated.

"Matteo went back to the house to call them," Elena said quietly. "Let's go back to the cart and wait."

She linked her arm through her husband's and gently guided him out of the woods toward the open field and the horse cart. Mario walked unsteadily, still reeling from what he had discovered. The dogs had stopped howling and were now barking as if in conversation about what they had found. Max handed the flashlight to Nico and wrapped his arm around Finley's shoulders as the cortege made its way back to the cart.

Shortly after they arrived, Elena pulled Mario into the driver's seat of the cart and plied him with more wine to ward off the shock that still seized him. She laid her head on his shoulder and held his glass of Chianti while he stared blankly into the encroaching night between sips. With her other hand, she clasped his folded hands in hers to stop the tremors that rocked them.

"I sent Sofia a message saying we would be late getting back, so she and Chuck would eat," Finley said, still resting in Max's arms as they leaned against the side of the cart.

Max nodded as a heavy silence enveloped them.

It was close to thirty minutes before the police arrived. Matteo led the cars along a side road just outside the well site that was wide enough to accommodate the cars. By then, the sun had dipped behind the hills, and a bright moon lit the fields.

Hearing the cars approach, Finley and Max walked back to the well, leaving Elena to tend to Mario. They reached the well just as Matteo alighted from the car with a man who appeared to be the officer in charge. The fast-flying instructions in Italian to the police who now combed the area ceased as the man greeted them.

"Hello. This gentleman says that you are visiting Americans. I hope you will excuse my bad English," he spoke in halting, heavily accented English. "My name is Officer Manzo. Francesco Manzo. I will be looking after this investigation."

Max extended his hand. "As Matteo may have said, I am Max Davies and this is my wife, Finley Blake. We are friends of the Fuscatis, here for a short truffle hunt."

"I am going to look at the scene, and then I will return to get a statement from you on what happened." The officer turned and walked back to the well, where his subordinates had set up barriers around the site.

Finley and Max withdrew to the periphery and stood with Matteo, Nico, and the dogs, which had quieted down and sat at their handlers' feet. As some of the police constructed a tent around the well and brought in auxiliary lighting, others went about erecting a pulley system to extract the body. Within minutes, they began to lower an officer with a camera into the well. A volley of Italian burst from the team as the pulley creaked, cameras flashed, and officers at the top pointed and exclaimed.

"What are they saying?" Finley whispered to Max.

"They're trying to get pictures of the scene down in the well before they attempt to bring her up. She is apparently partially wrapped in something—a tarp or blanket of some sort. They want to preserve as much of that as they can in case there is evidence on it."

As he spoke, the officer with the camera was pulled to the top and returned to terra firma. In his place, another officer in forensic overalls descended into the well. Alongside him, another harness was dropped into the black hole.

"How are they going to get her body up? That opening is so narrow. It must have been a very old well." Finley feared for Blaine in the confined space, even though she was dead. There was something vulnerable about the woman who had just hours before seemed so alive and now rested there.

"I suspect the guy they lowered is going to fit the harness around the body. They'll pull him up first and then lift her body out. The space isn't big enough for two."

"Do you think that man in the picture killed her?" Finley's words squeezed through the fear that gripped her throat. A tear slid down her cheek. She looked up at Max as her mind tried to piece together the time sequence of their encounter. "Who else could have done it?"

Max tightened his hold on her shoulder and kissed her forehead. "I don't know, darling. It looks so. You may have been in more danger than you knew."

It was close to nine o'clock when the police finished taking the statements of the group. Manzo had sent Blaine's body to the morgue in Spoleto and returned to surveying the scene. He released the foursome and the handlers after taking their statements with the proviso that they should not leave the area until allowed.

Mario had recovered from his shock and insisted on accompanying Max and Finley back to Sofia and Chuck's. "We can bring the wine and food that we didn't get to eat. And the truffles you found," Mario explained, holding up a bottle of Chianti that he then placed in the food hamper.

Elena patted his arm and, loath to further upset him, agreed to go as long as she drove. "You know you can't see well at night. And you've had quite a bit to drink already."

When they reached Chuck and Sofia's, all the lights were on, the house itself silhouetted in the moonlight against a now inky sky. Sofia greeted them at the door with a worried look. "What happened? Chuck is wild with speculation. He won't be able to sleep at all without an explanation."

Finley hugged her friend and kissed her cheek as she passed her the mesh bag with the truffles. "There is a lot to tell."

"At least you got to hunt before everything broke loose." Sofia, barefoot and dressed in a richly embroidered shirt and flowing black palazzo pants, led the way onto the patio, truffles in hand.

Chuck sat in the barrel chair, his guitar across his legs. "You had me so worked up, all I could do was play. If I never hear that 'Gran Vals' again, it will be too soon." He moved the guitar to its rest. "Now, tell me what the hell is going on."

While Elena and Sofia arranged the food from the hamper on the side table and pulled out plates and glasses, Mario, Max, and Finley recounted the events of the evening.

"Blaine is dead," Finley said softly. "We were so close to finding her, and now she's dead."

"Well, that should clear Grant, right? If she was killed today, he couldn't have done it. He was in jail." Sofia turned from arranging the food to address the group.

"It should, but who knows?" Max said. "We'll talk to his attorney tomorrow and give him the pictures with the time stamp to establish that she was alive earlier in the afternoon. Hopefully, that will help find the man in the pictures."

"He may be responsible for Blaine's death, but we have to find him to get the full story. Right now, it's all theory, and the police aren't going to take the time to see if it has legs or not," Finley said.

She took a gulp of the smooth wine and felt it wash down her gullet. She wanted to melt into the liquid and float away. And yet, however emotionally drained she felt by the whole ordeal, she had too many loose ends to walk away.

The phone in the kitchen interrupted her thoughts. Sofia went to answer it.

"Who's calling at this time of night? And on the house phone too," Chuck muttered. "If we were in the States, I'd say it was a spam call, but they don't have those here."

Sofia reentered the room, her brow wrinkled. "It's Assardi. He wants to speak to Finley."

Finley shrugged and went into the kitchen. She picked up the phone, an ancient push-button instrument from the last century, and spoke into the mouthpiece, "Hello? Mr. Assardi? What's happened?"

"Ms. Blake, sorry to bother you, but we have received some information from the coroner, and I wanted to talk to you about it. Tonight, if possible."

Finley wondered what could be so urgent as to require a visit tonight, but if it helped Grant, she would accede. "Certainly, we're all up. Please come over."

The group was on their second glasses of wine by the time the attorney arrived. He sidled in the door when Sofia greeted him, apologizing again for disrupting their evening.

"Nonsense! We are all too wound up to sleep, in any case," Sofia said as she led him onto the brightly lit terrace. "Can I get you a glass of wine? Or something nonalcoholic, perhaps?"

"Coffee, if you have it. It will be a long night."

Sofia headed into the kitchen, and Elena joined her.

"I won't keep you long. The body has been identified as Signora Lambert. The coroner also has some preliminary findings, and they are a bit disturbing," Assardi said.

"How so?" Max asked what Finley was thinking. "Do you have a cause of death?"

"The coroner says blunt force trauma to the back of the head."

"Do they know with what?" Finley probed.

Assardi shook his head.

"I'm confused. I know that being hit with a large object and dropped in a well is pretty gruesome, but I'm not understanding what is so disturbing as to have you here in the middle of the night." Finley tilted her head, perplexed.

The lawyer paused to accept the coffee Sofia handed him while Elena set a tray with a carafe and cups on the table. He raised the cup to his lips, his hand shaking as he sipped his coffee. He took his time returning his cup and saucer to the table, as if delaying the news as long as possible.

"Out with it, man!" Chuck demanded. "The woman's dead. What could be worse than that?"

"She was habitually abused," Assardi murmured quietly. "There is evidence of long-term physical abuse."

The room went quiet. Elena, Sofia, and Mario looked at one another in dismay. Chuck lasered in on Max, while Max turned to Finley. Finley stared straight ahead, her eyes unfocused.

When she didn't speak, Max asked Assardi, "What's the evidence of this abuse?"

The lawyer again took his time answering. "I know this must be a tremendous shock, but the coroner found bruises and scars on her wrists, evidence of several broken ribs, a slash mark on her leg. Things that he says suggest a history of physical abuse."

"Couldn't these have come from being dropped down a narrow well?" Finley had come back to life.

Assardi smiled sadly. "Some of the injuries were consistent with a fall from some distance, but others had healed over. They were from before the fall."

"That makes no sense." Finley shook herself to wake from the horrible dream. "Grant would never purposely hurt someone." She turned to Max. "You heard Mama and Daddy. He just doesn't have it in him."

Max took her hands and pulled her closer. "People change, sweetheart."

Finley took a deep breath and let it exhale into a long sigh. "So, what does this mean? Even if he is proven to be an abuser, he didn't kill her. We have proof that he was in jail at the time she was killed."

She went upstairs and retrieved her camera. She pulled up the relevant frames and showed them to Assardi.

"Who are these people?" the attorney asked.

Finley leaned over his shoulder, pointing out Blaine and the man with her. "That is the dead woman. She had the same clothes on when they found her, minus the hat. And that's the man you should be looking for."

"The police are working from the theory that the defendant had an accomplice. So just because he didn't kill her earlier doesn't mean that someone wasn't paid by Grant to kill her later."

Finley jumped up and started pacing. "Do you realize how absurd that sounds? Do you?"

Max raised his hand to slow her down, but she was already too worked up.

She continued. "Let's say that Grant *did* pay someone to bump her off. Where is he now? Is it this guy? He doesn't look like he's in any mood to knock her off anytime soon, does he?"

"Fin, sweetheart, calm down. The man is trying to help." Max tried to catch her eye.

Finley stopped her pacing and walked over to Assardi, who still held the camera. She tapped the screen gently. Her speech was moderated now.

"What this suggests to me is that his wife was having an affair. If he wanted to kill her for that, he failed, because as of one o'clock, she was still alive. And he was in jail for a murder that he never committed because that murder never happened. If the police want to do their job, they need to start looking for all the people she was in contact with between when this picture was taken and seven or seven thirty, when her body was found. Personally, I would start with this guy. His license plate number is in the next frame."

When she finished, Finley returned to her seat beside Max. He pulled her to him and kissed her hair.

"You make very good points, Ms. Blake. Unfortunately, that is not what the police think."

"Even when the facts refute their theory?" Chuck asked.

"They don't have this information, so they think Grant and an accomplice have killed her to keep her quiet about the abuse," the attorney declared. "I don't know how they will fit this information into that theory. We will see tomorrow."

Finley nodded. "Sorry to get so worked up, but to hang a man for murder, where I come from, the pieces have to fit. And they aren't here, even with the abuse charge included." She took the camera and headed toward the stairs. "Let me load these pictures on a drive for you. I was going to try to make them clearer, but there's no time for that now."

"Your wife is an attorney?" Assardi asked when she was gone.

"She trained as one but went into business instead," Max replied.

"She thinks like a lawyer! She raises some very good points. The abuse accusation aside, the timeline doesn't fit."

When Finley came down, she handed the attorney a thumb drive. "All of the pictures are there, including the one with this man's plate number. I think if you find him, you'll have your answers."

Assardi quickly finished his coffee and rose to leave. "I am sorry to upset you. I thought you needed to know. I will use these pictures to make tears—is that what you Americans say?—in their story."

Chuck laughed. "You mean 'shoot holes' in their story. Close enough! You got your work cut out for you, young man. Good luck."

Sofia escorted the lawyer to the door and returned to find the room cloaked in silence yet again.

Max was the first one to cut through it. His eyes sought Finley's, his voice comforting. "Fin, I'm not asking this to start a fight, and if you want to talk about it in private, I respect that, but I have to ask. Was there any evidence of abuse when you and Grant were together?"

Sofia jumped in. "You are among friends here, but if you want to answer Max in private, we understand."

Finley looked around the room at the sympathetic faces trained on her and smiled. "No, there was never any abuse in our marriage. Grant was controlling, wanted things a certain way for appearances' sake—how I dressed, the car we drove. But he never raised his hand to me. In fact, he rarely even raised his voice. It just wasn't something he would ever do. That's what's so puzzling."

Max embraced her. "Then we need to find the man in the pictures and ask *him* some pointed questions."

10

S LEEP DID NOT COME EASY to Finley that night. She had answered Max's question cavalierly based on what she knew of Grant, but as Max had reminded her several times since all of this began, that was some ten plus years ago. *People do change.*

Maybe Grant had taken to enforcing his controlling dictates physically. He had often grumbled under his breath when she had questioned or challenged him. Maybe he had tired of having his authority questioned and taken advantage of Blaine's petiteness. The uncertainty, the possibility that Grant had dramatically changed, had her tossing sleepless for most of the night.

When morning came, Max rose and got dressed, leaving Finley buried under the covers. She heard him reach under the bed frame for his shoes and felt his weight on his side of the bed when he sat down to slip them on.

"I know you're not sleeping," Max whispered over his shoulder. "You couldn't get to sleep if it was that or death."

"Aren't you kind!" Finley rolled over and followed the contours of his face with her eyes. The broadness of his forehead, the break at his brow, the slope of his nose . . . she was so lost in the beauty of his face that it took his hands on her cheeks and his lips on hers to bring her back to reality.

"Fin! Darling! Where'd you go?" Max was peering into her eyes. "You're punch-drunk, sweetheart."

"No sleep will do that to you."

Max rubbed her cheek gently. "And worry."

Finley threw back the covers. "And worry. I'll own it. I can't imagine it, but I have to. The coroner's preliminary report tells a sordid story I don't want to hear, but I have to face it."

Max walked around the bed and pulled her to him. "We'll talk to the coroner and Grant's attorney. And then you can talk to Grant. Don't draw any conclusions until then. You'll make yourself sick with suppositions and theories. Just wait for the facts."

They were out the door and on the road into Spoleto in fifteen minutes. Even Chuck could tell that Finley was in no mood for idle talk. Sofia packed up some bread and cheese along with a thermos of coffee and sent them on their way.

The photos laid out on the desk in Assardi's office were brutal to see. Much of the current cuts and bruises were from the woman being dropped, like a rag doll, thirty feet down the narrow well. The X-rays told a story of repeatedly broken ribs, a fractured clavicle, and a splintered forearm.

Finley sat speechless as the medical examiner, in fractured English, recounted the pattern of damage the pictures revealed. Max squeezed her hand when the doctor came to the conclusion that the tears on Finley's cheek indicated she had already drawn. "This woman was repeatedly abused. There is no doubt."

Assardi sighed and shook his head. "With the pictures of this woman and the man that you gave me earlier, I thought there was a chance to get Grant off. Even when we found her dead, there was doubt. He couldn't kill her from his jail cell. But now . . ."

"Now, the evidence says he's an abuser, but it still doesn't say he's a murderer," Finley pointed out. "I'm not defending him, but he was in jail when she was murdered."

"Yes, but the court will say that he hired someone to do it when he failed to kill her by pushing her off the train," the attorney opined.

"That doesn't make sense." Max knitted his brow. "I can't see how they can charge him with anything. The past abuse, while disturbing, wasn't responsible for her death. If it was a paid hit, where's the money trail? The police still need to find her killer."

"And they can start by looking for that man in the picture," Finley added.

The coroner had slipped out of the room and back to his caseload. Assardi resumed his seat at his desk. He shuffled the pictures around in front of him, picking up a photo before returning it to the desk without looking at it. Finally, he dropped his head in his hands.

Wearily, he said, "The police think that Grant was determined to see her dead, and when his way didn't work, he hired that man to seduce her and kill her."

"Let's leave off where he had time to do all this hiring and planning." Finley stared at the attorney. "Why? Why did he want her dead? And why now? Why bring her on holiday to kill her?"

"Because he had grown tired of her. Because he didn't want anyone to find out about the abuse." Assardi's voice rose in exasperation. "I don't know why. And quite honestly, at this point, the police don't care. They have their man, and they aren't going to let him loose. We may have had a chance before. But with the coroner's evidence, I don't think there is a snowman's chance in Hades."

Finley smiled at the malaprop but didn't have the energy to correct him. For what seemed like minutes but in reality was probably less than five seconds, the room was deadly silent. Assardi stared vacantly at the photos spread across his desk. Finley fixated on a point outside the window, somewhere beyond, and Max eyed her intently.

"I'm sorry." The lawyer's voice broke the silence.

In answer, Max and Finley rose and walked out.

Grant was by himself this time when they entered the visitor's room. He sat at a table near the window, the threads of light breaking through the wire mesh that encased it. He wore a short-sleeved black T-shirt that tugged around his torso and sweatpants that looked more like capris. In spite of the seriousness of the situation, Finley giggled to herself. *I guess it is hard to find clothes that fit a man who is almost six foot three inches tall.*

"The guards told me they found her. And then the coroner asked me to identify her," Grant said softly, skipping the formalities of a standard greeting.

Finley nodded and took the seat directly in front of him. Her stomach knotted at the sight of him, coiled in a mix of disgust and fear. "What are they saying?"

"That I killed her and dumped her in the well. That hanging was too good for me." Grant smiled sadly. "My Italian is getting pretty good."

"We've been to see your attorney. He knows that can't be true. You were in here when she died." Max lowered himself into a chair taken from the adjacent table. The guard frowned as if he was unsettled by the seating rearrangement, but he returned his eyes to staring straight ahead and remained silent.

"Did they say anything else?" Finley had been observing him fixedly since she and Max walked in. She had lived with this man for years, and yet she wasn't sure she knew anything about him. The photos said she had been living with an abuser. Had she also been living with a murderer, even if he had only planned the killing?

Grant shrugged. "Not really. The guards keep sneering at me, but they have been doing that since I got here. Have you heard anything else? If it's bad news, I would prefer hearing it from you."

"Where are Blaine's parents?" Finley redirected the conversation. Max shifted in the seat beside her, well aware that she was stalling.

"At the hotel, I presume. They were here yesterday morning. You saw them." Grant stared into a corner, his voice neutral until he started talking about his daughters. Then the anguish spurted out like a geyser. "Didn't say or do much besides chatter on about the girls. It broke my heart. I kept praying that they'd stop. Hearing about them and not seeing them is killing me."

When Grant dropped his head into his hands and started sobbing, Finley could only bring herself to glance over at Max. His face was as resolute as her heart. Just a few days ago, she would have attempted to comfort Grant, muttering empty words of solace, offering to help in some way. Today, she glared down at him stonily.

"Grant, did you ever beat Blaine?" Finley went straight for the jugular. She chose the word *beat* purposely, putting special emphasis on it when she spoke. She wanted a reaction. She waited for the recoil from the punch she knew she had landed on him.

"You believe it, too, eh?" Grant raised his head and muttered quietly, "I wondered when you would ask."

Surprised by Grant's reaction, Finley paused to reorder her thinking. Was he admitting it? What did he mean by *too*? Had Blaine's parents confronted him, as well?

"Grant, I asked you a basic question. Answer me yes or no." Finley took in a breath and held it while she waited for his answer.

"No. I never beat her. I never struck her." Grant's eyes welled with tears. "You know me. I couldn't do that."

"Then explain the pictures, the X-rays, the clear evidence of broken bones and scars. Help me understand, Grant!" Finley exhaled the hope she had been holding and leaned her body across the table. Her voiced pitched and almost broke before she dropped back and sighed. "Help us understand."

Grant straightened himself in the chair. He looked around the deserted meeting room. He closed his eyes tightly and began.

"She wasn't being abused. I was," Grant whispered.

Finley gasped and looked incredulously at Max. She shook her head slowly, as if shaking the loose pieces of her thoughts into logical place. But before she could speak, Max jumped in, his face locked into an angry scowl.

"You want me to believe that you, a healthy, grown man over six feet tall, were abused by that little sprite of a woman?" Max spat.

"That little princess could turn into a gremlin in a second. A Tasmanian devil who threw knives and pots, pulled down book-cases, shoved and punched and kicked. And all the while yelling the most hateful and hurtful things. It was living hell!" Grant scrunched his face as he spoke.

"Did you tell anyone? Say anything?" Finley watched the man shut his eyes tighter and contort his body, as if to avoid imaginary blows.

"Who would have believed me? You don't. No one can imagine the terror someone so angelic could deliver. I had to swear my doctor to secrecy."

"So, you have a record of this? Of the abuse?" Finley asked hurriedly, her voice almost at a whisper.

"Yes. A friend of mine who's a physician always cleaned my cuts and wrapped my ribs in private. He's set my nose twice. The last time, she broke four ribs and crushed my spleen with the cabinet she turned over on me. I ended up in the hospital." Grant opened his eyes and raised his shirt to show a set of jagged scars across his torso.

The guard, now used to unusual activity from Grant when Finley and Max were in the room, barely raised his head from his sporting news, but Finley and Max flinched in horror at the puck-ered skin of the scars against a bluish-gray background of tissue.

"Where were the children during all of this?" Finley asked frantically. "Goodness, tell me they weren't subjected to any of this."

"Blaine was smart. The girls were always over at a friend's house for a sleepover or at her parents' place for a visit when she would let loose on me. She didn't want to splash paint on the beautiful picture of domestic bliss that we'd created."

"Grant, why didn't you leave?" Finley couldn't conceive of living a duplicitous life in a house where people hurt her.

"Divorce would have destroyed me! All of this would have come out. The girls would have been scarred for life. My practice would have been ruined. My entire life would have gone up in smoke!"

"But, man, the house was already burning. How long did you think you could have gone on like this before one of you got seriously hurt or killed?" Max asked earnestly, his eyes locked on Grant's.

"I think the last time was a wake-up call for both of us. It was the worst." Grant closed his eyes again and rocked gently in his seat. "I wasn't sure I would make it out alive."

Grant stopped abruptly and put his head back in his hands. He breathed hard, a sorrowful moan escaping his lips. Finley and Max watched and waited. After several moments, he lifted his head and opened his eyes, but they were glazed as if transfixed.

"I can't really remember what set her off. It might have been about the affair. But she started screaming that I wasn't the father of the girls. Could never be. Then she started with the punching and hitting. She had a pot this time and kept hitting me with it."

Grant shook his head. "Then it got really serious. She grabbed a knife and started slashing, screaming what a sorry excuse of a man I was, asking why she ever married me. She charged at me a few times, stabbing one of the chairs and then the sofa.

"I held her off. Somehow I got the knife from her, but not before she sliced me on the arm." Grant adjusted his watchband absentmindedly and then ran his finger over a scar that ran up the side of his arm.

"It wasn't bad, only a few stitches, but there was blood everywhere. After she pulled the cabinet over, I picked her up and carried her into the bathroom, kicking, screaming, and cursing, and locked her in before I called my friend John. He came over, and we managed to wrestle her down so he could give her a sedative."

Grant went on. "John took me to the hospital. But he said if I didn't get her help, he would have her locked away. For the sake of the children, if nothing else. She agreed to start therapy. She even got on some meds. This trip was our new start."

"And then this," Finley murmured.

Grant nodded again, and his eyes refocused. He smiled sadly. "I don't think she ever meant to hurt me. She was mentally unwell. Something just snapped."

"Grant, you have to tell the police this. You can't keep this a secret anymore. From their vantage point, the bruising and scars on her body paint you as an abuser who was sick of his wife and plotted with a hired gun to kill her when chucking her from the train didn't work," Finley explained.

"And what part of my story should I use to refute that theory?" Grant laughed softly. "The part where I concede that I most certainly may have fractured her little arms at some point holding her off so she wouldn't stab me? Or would you prefer my saying that I might have broken a rib or two getting her into a strong enough hold so I could carry her to a safe place?"

Grant reached over and touched Finley's arm. "Let's face it. This is futile."

"Only if we quit," Finley said defiantly. She pulled out her camera and scrolled to a series of frames. She was waiting for the guard to protest her having the camera, but he continued reading his paper. "Take a look at these. Do you recognize this man?"

Finley decided not to show Grant the first picture in the series, of his late wife and the man kissing. He was already upset. Moreover, the shot was blurry, and both of the subjects' faces were hidden by the hat and the kiss. Finley scrolled past the next several frames until she reached a clear picture of the man standing at the mouth of the alleyway, looking back and forth. She leaned across the table and showed Grant the picture.

The intake of breath and the twitch of the eyebrow was subtle, so slight as to be almost imperceptible. But Finley saw it.

"Grant, you know this man. Who is he?"

Grant relaxed his shoulders before shrugging slightly again.

"Talk to me. You know this man. I can see it in your eyes. Dang it, tell me who he is."

Finley noticed a tinge of sadness color Grant's expression, but before he could answer, Finley heard a commotion outside the visiting room door. The guard put down his paper and headed toward the door. An elegantly dressed woman with a huffing man in tow behind her breezed past him and barreled toward the group seated at the table.

"You spineless waste of a man!" Beth Goddard spat out the rain of words like a barrage of bullets, each one targeted as she ran her eyes up and down Grant. "You killed my daughter. You beat her. You broke her. You killed her!"

Grant tried to break in, to refute the damning accusation. "I never struck Blaine. Never! I loved her."

"You lying bastard! Don't you ever speak the word *love* and my daughter's name together again. It's blasphemy. You are the devil incarnate!"

"Beth, Howard, you have to believe me. I didn't kill Blaine. I would never hurt her," Grant protested, tears running in rivulets down his cheeks.

"You can rot in hell as far as we care. If we were in the United States, we'd be sure they put a noose around your neck. But here, you'll just rot away like the vermin you are. Let your friends here pay to save you."

Grant was sobbing openly now. Beth stood over the weeping man as her husband glared in unbridled disgust. Finally, he spoke.

Pushing his wife out of the way, Howard bent low to whisper in Grant's ear. "Don't try to contact the girls. You are dead to them! Both you and Blaine died in a tragic accident, but your name will never be spoken in our house again. You're a ghost. Try anything to alter that, and I will bury you!"

11

EFEAT WRAPPED ITSELF AROUND FINLEY'S shoulders like a stifling cloak. It was evident from the hangdog way she walked back to the car with Max at her side. It surfaced again back at the house when she called to ask her father for his help in securing an attorney for Grant, now that the Goddards had withdrawn their financial and moral support.

"Girl, you tell me what you want me to do," her daddy had said when he and Mama got on the FaceTime call. "You still believe him, don't you?"

Finely had nodded, looking for support from Max. She had been so emotionally wrung out that at points in the conversation, she had gone silent. Max had filled in as he did now.

"There's no way he could have killed her, sir. The time sequence makes it impossible. He was in jail, but the police have their theory, and the abuse allegations have made them dig in their heels even more."

"Abuse allegations? What in heaven's name are you talking about?" Mama interjected.

Max looked at Finley, silently asking if she wanted to reveal this detail or if he should. Finley's weak smile was the green light for him to continue. "When they found Blaine's body, the coroner found evidence of past broken ribs and fractures not related to her death."

"Good God! They think Grant was a wife beater?" Mama's voice was barely a whisper.

Daddy growled. "And you want to keep helping this man? Finley, talk to me, girl. You can't condone this!"

"I don't. But Grant isn't the abuser. Blaine was. He has proof but has never said anything because of how it looks. Hercules against Betty Boop! Who would believe him? So he suffered in silence," Finley replied, her voice strong despite her flagging energy.

"Her scars were from him trying to hold her off. We saw his scars, as well. We'll check with his doctor friend who keeps patching him up, and the hospital records, but I tend to believe him, as does Fin, sir," Max added. "That said, the Italian police don't. And neither do his in-laws."

"They're going to try to take away his girls, Mama!" Finley cried. She explained the scene at the jail and the investigation leading up to that.

Daddy let out a deep sigh. "This is a mess. Let's take one step at a time. Should I be looking for a new attorney, or is the one he's got any good?"

"Assardi is good. He's smart and caring, and he's a fighter," Finley said. "If we can help him find the guy Blaine was with, he'll try to use that to raise enough doubt to get Grant released."

"Then that poor boy can fight to get his children back. However did this turn into such a hornet's nest? Why didn't he just leave her?"

"I asked the same question, Mama. But you know the answer as well as I. Appearances are everything to Grant. He has to control the narrative." Finley barely masked her disdain. "That's why I had to leave. I was being smothered. I couldn't live like that."

Daddy turned so that his face was full screen. His voice was gravelly. "Finley, I'm going to ask you this just once. I want an honest answer, and then I'll leave it alone. Did that man ever raise a hand to you? He didn't have to strike you. Did he ever raise a hand?"

Finley glanced over at Max and placed her hand over his. "Max asked the same question, Daddy. And no, Grant never, ever, raised his hand to me. As I told Max, he barely ever raised his voice. That wasn't—isn't—Grant. Which is why it is entirely plausible to me that he was the victim."

Her daddy nodded and then pushed the computer back so that Mama came onto the screen.

"Well, your daddy and I will pay his fees. You just tell his lawyer to prove his innocence so he can go home to his babies." Mama was emphatically shaking her finger at Finley. "And you, my girl, need to get some rest."

"I was going to do one better, ma'am, and take her into Siena later today. It's a nice day drive." Max kissed Finley's hand. "We'll grab a late lunch, take in a museum or two, and then head back."

"Sounds perfect. You two enjoy!" And with that, Mama and Daddy signed off.

Max pulled Finley to him and put his arm around her. Sofia had taken Chuck to his room for a nap after they returned from Spoleto and shared the drama of the morning. Finley and Max had retired to their own room while Sofia got Chuck settled. He had been too tired to do a truffle reconnaissance, so Sofia had encouraged Max to take Finley on an excursion.

"You feel up for a drive? We can postpone it if you'd prefer to rest." Max kissed her forehead as she nestled in his arms.

"A drive sounds like just the thing. I can always take a nap in the car." Finley pulled him in for a longer, more passionate kiss.

"Or we can while away the afternoon in here," Max said slyly as he returned the kiss.

Finley pushed away gently. "No way! You promised me Siena, so Siena it's going to be."

They were just leaving a message for Sofia when she joined them on the terrace.

"He's sleeping soundly now. It took him some time to fall asleep. Not a good ALS day today," she said sadly. "I'm glad you're heading for a drive. The sunset should be spectacular. Enjoy!"

Finley and Max kissed her gently and headed out. She was still waving as they drove off.

"I wish she and Chuck could have come with us." Finley looked back in the rearview mirror and saw that Sofia was gone. "Her life seems so lonely."

"Depends on how you look at it. I don't doubt that, at times, she'd like to get away from it all, but then being with Chuck was all she ever wanted, even when she was younger and could have done whatever she wanted. They decided against kids and are devoted to each other." Max smiled at Finley. "I think she's happy. She said as much."

"Well, he thinks she hung the moon and lit the stars." Finley chuckled. "You can tell by the way he looks at her."

"Don't I look at you the same way?"

"Indeed, you do. But you know I walk on water."

Max stifled a laugh. "I wouldn't go that far. But I do think you're something special!"

"I'm sorry that Grant wasn't so lucky. He really did love her." Finley frowned. "He was destroyed yesterday."

"Guess I would be too. Accused of a crime you didn't commit against someone you loved."

"And then to lose your children!"

Max and Finley were quiet for a few miles. The Tuscan hills, a distinctive sage and olive-green mix, rolled by as the latest Ed Sheeran song, "Eyes Closed," played on the radio. Finley sighed deeply.

"I hope the day gets better. I don't like being this depressed."

Max took her hand and kissed it. "It'll get better. We're going to have a relaxing day, wandering around the museums in Siena.

And while we're wandering, the solution to this whole puzzle will suddenly become clear, and all will be right with the world."

Finley scooted over in her seat to rest her head on Max's shoulder. A calm came over her as she took in visual gulps of some of the most scenic countryside in the world in the company of the man she loved above all others. She grabbed the mental lifeline Max had thrown her and hung on. "You promise?"

"Promise."

Finley had to admit that she felt like a schoolgirl on a grand tour following behind Max as he led her through the streets of Siena. It was too early for the Palio, the famous horse race that took place in the Piazza del Campo every year, but there were enough architectural wonders to have her oohing and aahing as narrow cobbled streets opened to structural marvels like the Siena Cathedral and the Torre del Mangia.

They had settled on the Pinacoteca Nazionale, the main museum of Sienese art in the city, as the one museum they would tour on this trip. But Finley had changed the rules midstream and insisted on a quick walk through the Museo dell'Opera Metropolitana, one of the oldest private museums in Italy, when they finished at the Pinacoteca.

"They say they have a couple of Titians among the paintings on the upper floors that are worth seeing," Finley noted as she pulled Max up the marble stairs of the central exhibition area.

Housed in three rooms on the top floor, the paintings in the collection were not extensive, but they offered breathtaking examples of the artistry of Medieval and Renaissance Italian painters. A series of oils on wood boards caught Finley's eye. Sketches for Titian's great work, *Diana and Actaeon*, they depicted the legend of Actaeon coming upon Diana and her nymphs. A man catching a glimpse of the beauty of the goddess and her handmaidens while they bathed.

Finley was transfixed by the detail in each subject's expression, the positioning of the bodies that showed emotion and movement, the story that Titian, with carefully placed strokes, was able to tell. It took Max giving her several nudges before she was able to tear herself away from the paintings.

"Fin, sweetheart, I know you're enjoying this, but I'm hungry. That bread and cheese wore off an hour ago," Max whispered.

Finley refocused on his face. "Now that you mention it, I'm a little peckish too. Let's go, then."

At the suggestion of one of the guards at the museum, they wandered across the plaza and down a few narrow alleys until they reached Antica Osteria Da Divo, a gem of a restaurant tucked away off the street. Finley and Max were led through a stone arch to a table in the nave. Open stone walls, some that looked like they dated from the Renaissance, surrounded them on all four sides. Above, the ceiling vaulted into a lattice of heavy, hewn-log beams.

"I remember this part of town from my honeymoon trip." Finley chuckled at the irony. "I think there is a pizza place that we went to with a stone oven not far from here."

"You and Grant came here for your honeymoon?"

Finley nodded. "Yes, we started in Dubrovnik and then went to Venice, Florence, and Rome. Siena and San Gimignano were a couple of the day trips we took."

"That's a pretty impressive itinerary." Max studied her over the top of his menu. "We never really had a honeymoon, did we?"

"Our whole time together has been one big honeymoon, if you think about it." Finley reclined in her chair and gazed at him as she took a sip of the floral Falanghina the waiter had set in front of her. "Morocco, London, Zanzibar, India, Palawan . . . Places most people choose for a honeymoon destination, we've strung together into one big lifetime journey."

Max leaned forward and kissed her hard. "And I wouldn't want to take it with anyone but you. But that said, we do need to go on a real honeymoon. Somewhere we can make memories."

"I think our travels have been quite memorable. Stuff we can tell our grandkids." Finley grinned teasingly when she mentioned progeny, a subject that was frequently woven into their recent conversations. She eyed him pensively. "But if we were to take a *real* honeymoon, where would you want to go?"

He had surprised her by talking about wanting to take a honeymoon. A man who had been so resistant to the whole institution of marriage was now swept up in the trappings. Was he jealous of what she had had with Grant, or just committed to making sure that the two of them had stories they could recall fondly when they were old and gray?

"I'm not sure. But you're right. We've gone to many of the exotic honeymoon locations. Maybe someplace closer to home. A castle stay in Dublin or maybe Edinburgh?" Max said.

"Or a cabin in the Alps or a houseboat up the Seine?"

"So many options!" Max tore off a piece of soft bread and dipped it in olive oil. He chuckled as he chewed. "Maybe that's why we haven't gone on a honeymoon trip. We don't want to have to decide."

For the next several minutes, they enjoyed their lunch and each other's company. They and another nicely dressed gentleman were the only other patrons inside the restaurant. The other guests sat outside, enjoying the sunshine.

As Finley took another bite of her *malfatti*, spinach and Sienese gnocchi with ricotta and Parmesan, a thought occurred to her. "Max, do you think Grant knows the man in the picture is the guy who's having an affair with his wife?"

"What do you mean?" Midway to his mouth, Max paused his forkful of *pici*, the handmade pasta unique to Siena with a wild boar ragu. "He talked about an affair. So he must have known she was seeing someone."

"Yeah, but did he know who?"

"I'm not following you."

"Grant recognized that man. I know he did. He flinched at the image with a strange look on his face. But why? What was he reacting to?"

"Maybe he was reacting to the prospect that his wife, whom he was trying to start over with, might have left him."

"Maybe. All I know is something isn't adding up. We need to talk to Grant again."

12

BY THE TIME MAX AND Finley returned to Spoleto, visiting hours at the jail were almost over. The guard, intent on going home to a nice home-cooked dinner perhaps, was none too pleased at their last-minute entrance. He grumbled under his breath as he slunk down the hall to get Grant and lead him into the meeting room.

"You have twenty-five minutes!" he barked in Italian as he took up his position along the wall. "Twenty-five."

Grant struggled to contain his surprise at the visit. "Didn't expect to see you here again. I figured you had bailed on me as well." He slumped in the chair, his shoulders rounded.

"Your attorney should be over to see you tomorrow. Daddy and Mama are picking up the bill," Finley announced when she and Max sat down. "I figured you wanted to continue with Assardi. Let me know if you want to switch so I can let them know."

Grant wrinkled his forehead and ran his hand through his hair. "Finley, why are you and your family doing this? It's hopeless."

"Only if we give up. You know you're innocent. Max and I don't think you killed her, and Mama and Daddy share that view. So the only rub is to find the evidence that supports that belief." Finley pulled her camera from her bag. "We don't have a lot of time, so you stonewalling me isn't helping your case."

Max jumped in while Finley scrolled through the frames, looking for the photos she needed. "When Finley showed you the picture of the man who we think may have been involved in all of this, you reacted."

The set of Grant's jaw said he wasn't going to confirm or deny Max's statement. Max soldiered on. "Grant, you know that man. I don't know in what context, but you recognized him. Stop BSing us."

"Is this the man Blaine was having an affair with? Is this what set her off last time? Is this why she wanted to stab you? Because you found out, and you argued with her about it?" Finley turned the camera to show the picture of the man at the mouth of the street, the same shot she had shown him that morning.

Grant glanced at the picture briefly before looking away, his mouth pinched and pained. But Finley was determined not to let him off the hook. She pulled up a shot of Blaine and the man kissing and stuck it in his face. Blurry though it was, it was still clear enough for recognition.

"Because this is the same man who was kissing your wife just a few days ago. You can deny it all you want. The truth isn't going away. You know this man. You know him!"

Grant turned away suddenly, his back toward the camera. His breathing quickened, and he clenched and unclenched his fists, his jaw working back and forth to defuse the tension.

Finley pulled up another picture of the twosome locked in an embrace. Again, she thrust the camera in his face. "What's his name? How do you know him?"

She watched his reaction carefully, his refusal to engage. Running out of time and desperate for any information he might let slip, she changed tactics.

"We have it all wrong, don't we?" she said softly. "Blaine wasn't angry about you finding out about her affair. She was angry when she found out about yours, wasn't she?"

Grant turned and glared at her with a look that would freeze blood. *Finally, a reaction.* She had only another five minutes before visiting hours were over. Five minutes to squeeze out the information that might save him from years in jail.

"You found out about her lover, and she searched out yours? Did she make you promise to end it?" Finley's voice was low, a mix of enticing and threatening. She drew her lips into a wry smile. "Did you ask the same of her? Did she promise to put it behind her and then lie? How did that make you feel?"

Grant cried out under the relentless questioning. "I didn't kill her! I wouldn't."

"Then give us the name of the man who did. You know him. This is Blaine's lover, isn't it? The man you found out about! Tell us his name!" Finley countered. "Grant, you're going to go to jail for the rest of your life. You're going to lose your girls if you don't start talking. Talk to me!"

The guard started toward them. Their time was up. Grant preempted the guard's interruption of the interrogation by standing and walking toward the door. He ignored Finley's demand; he ignored her. He kept his gaze fixed straight ahead, his long, lanky frame ramrod straight as he walked through the door and down the hall to his cell.

"Why won't he talk? Why? He knows that man. I know it." Finley was fit to be tied by the time she got to the car. She had stalked out of the police station, slamming the door so hard, the desk officer looked up from his newspaper and shook his head. Max followed her out, apologizing to those in her wake.

"Fin, you're going to have a stroke. Calm down, sweetheart." Max drew alongside her when she finally stopped in front of their car and leaned against it, her arms crossed tightly in front of her. He paused for a moment before pulling her to him and kissing her nose. "I know you're frustrated, but you can't force him to talk."

"But why is he evading us? If that man killed her, wouldn't he want him to pay for what he did?"

Max pushed away to catch her eye. "Unless he was the one who paid that man to kill her."

Finley sighed in defeat. "You think he's involved, don't you?"

"Sweetheart, I'm trying to figure out why he isn't trying to save himself. You're fighting harder to free him than he is. Why? It may be that he didn't think he would get caught, and now you have him in the crosshairs."

"But he keeps saying he didn't do it."

"He would, wouldn't he? He's trying to save his skin."

"No, it's something else. His protests are anguished, not defiant. The only thing defiant is his refusal to say who that man is. We have to find out. We have to call Evans," Finley said, opening the car door quickly and sliding inside.

"Evans? Not sure I understand?"

"Yes, Evans. We'll send him the picture, and he'll get a name for us. He has ways we can only imagine."

"Ways I don't want to know about. But you can talk to Evans this time!" Max stressed with a wry smile.

Finley appreciated the brief moment of humor. She was spent, thoroughly exhausted from trying to get Grant to talk. She didn't know how investigators and police officers kept up the pace. She guessed if she were a police officer, she would have buckled under the daily grind of pumping suspects for information. She was almost ready to throw in the towel now. But the prospect of Grant's children thinking their father had done something he hadn't was too much. She had to clear him for their sakes.

Finley pulled Evans's number from her contacts, even before they started back to the house. The number rang several times before Evans picked up.

"Finley? Everything all right?" Evans's deep voice echoed in the closeness of the car's interior.

"Yes, we're both fine." Finley sighed and hurried on, the words tumbling over one another as she spoke. "But Grant isn't. I think Max texted to let you know that they found his wife's body. And we got a picture of the man she was with shortly before she died. We showed the picture to Grant. He recognized the man. We know he did, but he won't tell us his name. Can you help us?"

Finley could hear Evans moving around in the background. "I should have asked whether this was a good time to talk," she added.

Knowing Evans, he might have been deep undercover with a gun pointed at him by a suspected money launderer or doing hand-to-hand combat with a knife-wielding villain when the phone rang. Seeing it was Finley, he would have, of course, taken the call.

Evans laughed. "Yes. It's fine. I'm just thinking."

Finley glanced at Max and shrugged. They would have to keep waiting until Evans had processed the information she had shared.

"Can you send me the picture?"

"Sure. I sent it a few seconds ago," Finley replied. "It should be clear enough for you to do an identification."

"I've got it," Evans said. "I need to run, but I'll get somebody working on it and get back to you. It may be a day or two before I can contact you, though."

"Thanks. And no problem. We'll be here." Finley stared at the phone as the call clicked off and whispered sadly, "Hopefully, Grant will be too."

It was dark by the time Finley and Max turned onto the lane that led to the house. The lights on the terrace and in the front hallway were on, but the rest of the house was dark. Tired and ready for a drink, they dropped their backpacks at the foot of the stairs and headed toward the kitchen.

Finley opened the bread box and tore off a portion of crusty bread, which she placed on a plate with the dried meats and wedge of Parmesan she had taken from the larder. Max, in the meantime, had poured a glass of a local white for Finley and a rich Chianti for himself. They had just shut the kitchen light off and were headed toward the terrace when Sofia met them in the hallway.

"I thought I heard something out here." She greeted them with a kiss. "Did you have a pleasant trip?"

Max passed Sofia his glass of wine and went back to the kitchen for another pour while Finley began to recount the highlights of their excursion to Siena.

"Siena was as lovely as I remembered. Grant and I visited before, when we were on our honeymoon," Finley said.

"Had you really? I didn't know that," Sofia said with a note of surprise.

"I didn't either," Max said as he came back into the room, wine bottle in hand.

"You make it sound like it was some sort of conspiracy!" Finley wiggled her eyebrows and curled her lips like a comic strip villain. "It was nothing of the sort. Max, you suggested Siena, not me."

"I was a total innocent. I didn't know the place had history for you," Max teased.

"No history, just a few memories," Finley responded. "We had lunch at a great restaurant around the corner from the cathedral—"

"Antica Osteria Da Divo. It was superb!" Max added. "Have you been there?"

Sofia shook her head. "We may have, but I don't think so. And we don't get out much now."

"Well, if you want to meet friends for lunch while we're here, we'll be more than happy to look after Chuck. Chuck can play for us," Max offered.

Finley hoped that Sofia would take her up on the offer. The woman needed to get out on her own from time to time, or the responsibility of looking after Chuck would weigh her down. If that happened, she would be no good to Chuck or herself.

"I may take you up on that," Sofia said. "Any news on Grant's case?"

"Not really." Finley glanced at Max, who gave her an encouraging smile.

"We showed Grant a picture of the man who was with Blaine and asked if he knew the guy. He claimed not, but his body language said otherwise," Max said. "Finley pressed him hard, but he denied knowing him."

"Maybe he was reacting to the fact that his wife was having an affair," Sofia suggested. "I would guess seeing your wife with another man could be upsetting."

"Even before I showed him the one with them kissing, there was a flicker of recognition," Finley declared. "He's shutting down on us, and I don't know why."

"There may be a few reasons he doesn't want to acknowledge the man. One is what I said earlier—he is in denial. Then again, he may know the man as the one he hired to kill her, and now he is regretting it," Sofia conjectured.

"Well, denial isn't going to get him out of jail, and I seriously doubt Grant hired a hit man." Finley was up and pacing now. She was getting angry all over again at Grant's intransigence. They had come so close to raising the doubt necessary to free Grant, and yet he wasn't trying to help his cause.

"What are you going to do now?" Sofia asked. Her face softened as she glanced between Finley's frustrated pacing and Max's understanding calm.

"I'm going to distract this caged tigress before she pops a blood vessel. We're going to go to a couple of the vineyards I noticed on the way back from Siena. Maybe a tour and a tasting will calm her down." Max pulled Finley close when she stopped her pacing and dropped down onto the seat beside him.

"Max is right. We might as well go on a wine tour. I'm only going to end up frustrated if I stick around waiting for Grant to talk." Finley leaned back in Max's arms and sighed wearily. After a moment, she sat up suddenly. "Hey, why don't you and Chuck come with us?"

Max nodded his agreement. "Great idea! I think Chuck's chair will fit in the trunk of the little car, so he doesn't have to drive. And we can find wineries that have wheelchair access. What do you think?"

Sofia's face brightened. "If he rests today, he might be good with an excursion. We can see tomorrow morning, but I think it might work."

Finley hadn't seen Sofia this excited since their arrival. A glass-half-full sort of woman by nature, Sofia had put on a good show, but the last couple of days, when Chuck's energy had waned markedly, had worn on her. Finley prayed that Chuck felt well enough to go along.

While Sofia and Max discussed which wineries to tour the next day, Finley found a corner on the terrace that offered decent light in the deep night cover. She went to the favorites list on her phone and scrolled down to her sister's number. Whitt would help her make sense of this morass Grant was trying to drown himself in. If nothing else, she would tell her something crazy that David had done and have Finley holding her sides with laughter. And for that brief moment, all the anxiety around Grant's fate would be gone.

"Hello?" David's welcoming voice greeted her before his image came on the screen. A devilishly handsome man with a dark reddish-blond mop of hair that half covered a pair of killer blue eyes, David had an easy charm that was a perfect counterpoint to her sister's irreverent manner and rapier tongue.

"Hey, little brother. How's it going?"

"Finley! What's up? Where are you? Max with you?"

"Max and I are in Spoleto. Something came up, and we're trying to get it sorted. Have you talked with Mama lately?"

"Not since earlier in the week. We've been up visiting my family outside Telavi. Reception sucks, so she might have tried to call. We just got back." Finley remembered the family vineyard that his mother's side of the family owned in the wine-making region of Georgia.

She could hear David moving around and hoarsely whispering to Whitt.

"I'm getting Whitt so you can fill us in at the same time," David said after a couple of seconds of silence.

"Okay, so what have you gotten yourself into this time?" Whitt joked when she came into view. She was a pretty woman, fine-featured with chestnut-brown hair that she wore dead-straight and parted in the middle and piercing green eyes. "I thought leaving you with Max would keep you safe, but *no!*"

"Give me a break. It's not me in trouble this time. It's Grant," Finley quipped.

"Grant, your ex?" Whitt exclaimed, looking at David quizzically. "What happened?"

"He called out of the blue, saying he needed help. He was in an Italian jail, charged with murdering Blaine."

"His Barbie doll wife?" Whitt asked. "Why would he want to kill her when he could just ignore her and save the jail time? That's what most upper-class husbands do, isn't it?"

"Whitt, be kind. Grant's really in trouble." Finley recounted the events of the last several days, especially her conversation with Grant in the past several hours. "He's refusing to identify a guy who I know he knows. I could kill him for shutting down on me."

"Sorry he's being such a pain. You know he was never my favorite person." Whitt smirked.

"You and Daddy!"

"That said, I don't want to see him hang, so what can we do to help?" Whitt said.

"I don't know. What am I missing?" Finley implored. "What would make him clam up like that?"

13

INLEY HAD SPENT ANOTHER HALF hour talking to her sister. Whitt, spurred on by David at times, spouted off a list of reasons why Grant might be reticent to talk.

"Have you considered that he might have done it?" Whitt proffered with a raised brow.

"How? She was alive when they threw him in jail. He couldn't have killed her."

"Then he hired someone," David interjected.

"And the guy in the picture is the hit man? I don't think so." Finley had sent Whitt and David several of the pictures to get their reaction. "This is personal. Real personal. I have been over this so many times. I need a new angle. Help!"

"What about this? We've established that both Blaine and Grant were having affairs, right?" Whitt started scribbling on Post-it notes and placing them around her kitchen, where she and David were taking the call.

"I put it out there, and he didn't deny it, so I guess that's a fair assumption. At least for now."

"So what if he knows the guy because the guy is the husband of the woman he's seeing?" Whitt strutted back to the screen after slapping another sticky note on the wall. She wore a self-satisfied grin, emphasizing her triumph with swish of her hip and a snap of her fingers. "Describe his reaction again."

"It was really subtle the first time. He inhaled quickly, and his eye twitched before he relaxed his body and tried to look normal. And then all the other times, he just turned his back, like he didn't want to see it."

"Yep, I bet you that's it. What can you find out about this guy? Is he Italian or foreign?" Whitt had taken a seat beside David.

"He said he only spoke Italian, but I didn't believe him. We asked Evans to see what he could find on him."

"You roped Evans into this? How'd that happen? How is he, by the way?"

Finley laughed. Both sisters had always had a soft spot for the ruggedly handsome inspector.

"He's fine. Someplace secret doing something we aren't supposed to know about," Finley hinted. "But truth be told, it wasn't me who got Evans involved. It was Max."

"Max? Why? He would have been the last one I would have thought of to bring Evans in." Whitt shook her head and looked at David, surprised. David also looked incredulous.

"He needed a sanity check after the conversation with Mama and Daddy, and Evans was the sanest person Max could think of at the time."

"That's an understatement," Whitt quipped.

"In any event, Evans is checking the guy out. It would be too much of a coincidence if Grant and Blaine were involved with a husband and wife. Ew! That's more than a bit sordid, if you ask me."

"Maybe, but I bet that's why he reacted like he did. If Evans confirms it, you owe me dinner!"

"I still think it's a bit far-fetched, but if Evans says you were right, dinner it is," Finley said. "Look, I better hop off. Thanks for the ideas. Good to see you guys. Love you!"

Max refilled her glass when she rejoined the conversation. "Whitt?"

"Yeah. She thinks Grant knows the guy because he's the husband of the woman he's having an affair with. I say it's too much of a coincidence." Finley dropped into the seat beside Max and snuggled up to him.

"Maybe, but maybe not." Sofia considered what Finley had said as she took a sip of her wine. "I remember when we were in New York, the circle of people we knew was small, and some of the couples were mixing around."

Finley's eyes grew large. "Really?"

"Not my cup of tea by a long shot, but I've heard a few similar stories. It isn't all too uncommon," Max said. "The group that Grant runs with in the city might have thought nobody would find out—until now. Maybe that's why he's so closemouthed."

"Who knows? And for now, who cares? Did you guys find some wineries with a ramp for Chuck?" Finley asked.

Max and Sofia both nodded. "Just hope he's up to it tomorrow," Sofia said.

Chuck was more than up for an outing when Finley and Max came down for breakfast. He was dressed and sitting in his barrel chair on the terrace. He kissed Sofia when she handed him what appeared to be his second cup of coffee.

"So which ones are we going to?" he asked as Max and Finley came onto the terrace.

"Good morning." Max shook Chuck's hand before leaning over to give Sofia a peck on the cheek. "You're up and raring to go, I see."

"Yeah. Sofia said you wanted to go tasting. There're quite a few that we've visited that can handle my chair," Chuck said. "That is the one thing I would have had a hard time giving up—my wine tours."

Sofia laughed. "You most certainly would have been a grumpy man without a few trips to the vineyard. Even with Amata and Silvano bringing you bottles." She patted Chuck's hand. "Max and I reviewed a few last night. We put in a surprise for you!"

"A surprise? Impossible! I know all the vineyards," Chuck protested.

"Do you really?" Sofia teased.

All during the trip out to Montalcino, Chuck, who was riding shotgun, kept asking where they were headed. He knew the countryside like the back of his hand, so he was puzzled when Max turned onto a back road that cut between fields of grapes. On either side of the main road, there was row upon row of green vines trellised on lines that laced the hillsides. At the end of each row of grapes, roses had been planted. Finley had seen this in the Loire Valley.

"What are the roses for? I thought French winemakers were the only ones that did that," Finley asked.

Chuck nodded toward Sofia. "The lady here is the expert on making the stuff. I just drink it!"

Sofia laughed. "I am hardly an expert, but some things I know. I think it is a pretty common practice across the world, even though the French like to think they're the only ones who do it. The roses attract bees, which you need for pollination. But the aphids also like their sweetness, so the roses get attacked before the vines do."

"Like an early warning system to protect the vines," Max said.

"Exactly. It is an age-old practice that my grandfather used to use," Sofia confirmed. "He said it also kept the horses working the vineyards from cutting the turn too close at the end of the row—they'd get pricked!"

"Goodness. I never thought of that," Finley said, drawing back as if to avoid imaginary thorns.

They continued along for a few minutes before Chuck could hold his tongue no longer. "Do you know where you're going?"

Max shrugged nonchalantly before giving Chuck a side-glance. "I think so. It's what GPS said to do."

"GPS wouldn't know its way around a slice of bread if the 'Over' sign was facing up," Chuck grumbled. "Tell me where you want to go, and I'll get you there."

"If we tell you, it wouldn't be a surprise," Max countered. For a moment, Chuck was silent.

When they reached a fork in the rutted road they were following, Finley pointed left. The path snaked around the base of two bright green hills that were striped with rows and rows of closely planted vines.

They reminded Finley of the tea terraces she had seen in Sri Lanka when she'd traveled with her sister a few years ago—a sea of green. In Nuwara Eliya, the sisters had also found a body, but in a tea dryer, not a well. Evans had been involved then. She wished he were more closely involved this time. Maybe he could still shine a light on the darkness of Grant's case before it was too late.

After several minutes, Max pulled up before an ancient-looking stone house with blue-green shutters. Over the front door and much of the graveled yard, a large pergola draped with grapevines stood. A squat, middle-aged woman in a navy floral-patterned housedress came to the door. The ties of her apron stretched to reach around her.

"*Benvenuto!* Welcome!" The woman wiped her hands on the apron and came around to Chuck's side of the car. Sofia had hopped out to open Chuck's door while Max pulled the wheelchair from the trunk.

It took Chuck next to no time to pull his wheelchair out and slide himself into it. He turned to the woman and shook his head. "I should have known you were behind this surprise! Aurelia

Conti, meet my friends, Finley and Max. Max and I go way back to my New York days."

Aurelia stepped forward to give Chuck a peck on both cheeks before doing the same to the rest of the group.

"I hope you will excuse my English." Aurelia dipped her head shyly. "I am so happy for you to come and visit us. Banfi, the castle, and its vineyards are well-known. I hope you will take a tour. But before, we want you to taste some special wines."

She led them into the house through one door and back out into the pergola through another door that was adjacent. A modern hog-wire fence separated the terrace from the graveled driveway.

"We had to put this in when we started bringing the dogs down to this area of the grounds. They were puppies and liked to wander." She opened her arms to show the expansive area that surrounded the house. "If they got out, we would never find them. Now they are big and can go everywhere."

"So how far are we from the castle?" Max asked as Aurelia motioned for them to sit. A handsome young man in his early twenties entered the terrace, carrying a tray of wines, and set them in front of Aurelia.

"Less than a kilometer on the other side of the hill. This building used to be the caretaker's cottage, but we took it over for private tastings."

After the specially curated tasting, which included some of the vineyard's vintner reserves along with local cheeses, dried meats, and fresh strawberries, cherries, and figs, Chuck was ready to take a short rest.

While Chuck slept and Sofia savored a glass of her favorite Poggio all'Oro, Max and Finley decided to take a walking tour of the castle grounds. The path up the hill to the castle wound through fields that alternated the green of the vines with the blond of ripe wheatgrasses. In the near distance sat a cluster of connected stone buildings capped by a tower that looked over miles and miles of the Tuscan countryside.

"The castle, I presume." Max paused in the middle of the road to take in the view. "I don't know what I was expecting, but this seems like of more a manor house than a castle."

"I think you are only seeing a piece of it, from the narrow end." Finley pointed to the long side of the edifice that stretched for what looked like a mile.

"Oh, that looks much more impressive." Max followed her line of sight.

"I think we are on the back side. Let's walk around and approach it from the gateway."

As Finley had expected, the view of the castle walking through the wrought-iron gates toward the main entrance was magnificent. Sentinels of Italian cypress lined the entry road for almost a mile before giving way to the iron gates that now stood open. The road continued into a graveled yard that finally led to a flagstone-tiled driveway and entry terrace.

"Now, this is more like it." Max stepped back to allow Finley a clear photograph of the entry to the castle. "We were approaching it through the back door."

"Feel better now?" Finley laughed. "Shall we grab another glass of wine before we head back to Chuck and Sofia?"

"Yeah, let him sleep another half hour or so."

"And give Sofia some quiet time."

They entered the outdoor patio that overlooked a Tuscan patchwork of greens and browns. Choosing a table close to the overhang, they ordered a Rosso di Montalcino for Max and a San Angelo Pinot Grigio for Finley. While they waited for their wines, Finley pulled out several postcards from the museum in Siena, the ones of Titian's *Diana and Actaeon*, and placed them on the table.

"What are those?" Max pulled the cards closer and scanned the pictures. "These from Siena? Pretty."

Finley brought one of the cards closer and looked at its detail before pushing it back to Max. "They are of his sketches for the painting. Look at the cards closely and tell me what you see."

She waited, sipping the wine that had just been served, as Max ran his eyes over every inch of the three cards in from of him.

"That you bought three of the same painting?" Max ventured, an eyebrow raised.

"Look at them again. Closely."

"I thought I already did. Can you give me a hint?" Max picked up one postcard, took a sip of his wine, and studied the image again. After several minutes of concentrated review of the cards again, he placed them back on the table. "Sweetheart, they all look the same to me. Sorry."

Finley smiled and shook her head. "It took me a while, too, but then it seemed so obvious, I couldn't believe I had missed it."

She laid the cards out in a row in front of Max and then pointed to a figure behind the screen that claimed the center of the tableau in each of the sketches they had seen at the museum in Siena just days before. "What is Actaeon staring at?"

Max's mouth flew open as he drew each of the cards to his eyes and then put them back on the table.

"Max, dearest, we have to talk to Grant again."

By the time they reached the house and dropped off Sofia and Chuck, late afternoon was easing into evening. The sky was painted the dusty indigo that twilight had made its signature color when Max and Finley started for the police station. Max had called ahead so that Grant would be waiting for them.

"Max, would you mind terribly if I spoke with Grant alone? I think it might be easier." Finley watched Max's face for a reaction.

"No, I don't mind. I can sit in the lobby and hassle the desk officer." Max grinned maliciously. "Don't be too hard on him. This must be difficult."

Finley sighed. She steeled herself for Grant's reaction to the conversation. She ran over in her mind what she would say, how she would phrase it, how she would react to another round of stonewalling. How she would ease the truth out of him. The truth that might set him free.

Grant was sitting in the usual place at the same table when she walked in. The rest of the tables were empty. The same guard was leaning against the wall. From the expression on his face, the guard had given up wondering why she kept coming back, trying to save a man the police knew was a murderer. Silly woman.

She slid into the chair and took a few breaths to calm herself under Grant's watchful eye.

"Where's Max? He's given up on me too?"

"He's outside. I wanted to talk to you alone."

"What about? I don't know any more than I told you before. And I doubt there is any new evidence, or my lawyer would be here, not you. So . . ." Grant sighed. His lips twisted into a resigned smile as he leaned back in the chair. "Sorry I got you involved in this."

Finley wasted no time. "Well, I am involved, so let's cut the crap. Grant, you know that man, the one in the pictures, don't you? You know him *very* well." She was direct, but she kept her voice low and soothing.

"Are we going over this again?" Grant straightened himself in the chair and glared at her. "What's the point?"

"The point is that that man wasn't just Blaine's lover, was he?" Finley punctuated each word even as she kept her voice low. Then she paused. She wanted him to say it, not her.

Instead, Grant's jaw tightened, but he remained silent.

Damn it, man. Help me find this man. He may have killed your wife. Admit that you know him. You know him very well. He isn't worth hanging for.

"Grant, what's his name? Tell me how you know him," Finley coaxed. "He was your lover, too, wasn't he?"

Grant pushed back his chair suddenly, almost knocking it over. The guard glanced over but didn't move. He was used to these outbursts by now. Even so, he kept his eye on Grant as he moved to the far side of the room and stood staring out into the darkness.

Finley saw his hands clench into fists for a moment before they released and hung at his sides. She didn't follow him. She sat and waited. Waited until he was ready to say the words that might start to untangle the mess he had gotten himself into. She watched the digital clock on the wall tick off the minutes. Three. Five. Ten. Twelve.

Just as the numbers on the clock changed again, Grant turned and walked back to the table.

"I need to stop lying to save face and start telling you the truth. He isn't worth rotting in jail for. How did you know?" He searched her face for answers. "Yes, Marc was my lover, but I didn't know he was Blaine's too."

14

IT TOOK SOME TIME FOR Grant's revelation to sink in fully. Finley and Max walked up to the trattoria where they often took their morning coffee. The owner was milling around the restaurant, talking to patrons, when they walked in. He showed them to a small table in the back and took their drink order. They sat silently while they waited to be served. This time, Finley spoke first, as soon as the waiter delivered their wines.

"What does this change in the equation? How can we use this to punch holes in the police theory?" she whispered, looking around cautiously to be sure no one in the crowded space heard her.

"I'm not sure it does. They are working from the assumption that Grant hired someone to kill Blaine. From Grant's reaction, this guy Marc wasn't the hit man. So, if he did hire someone, we are no closer to finding out who the hit man was."

"The whole hit man theory doesn't hold water for me. The timing is wrong." Finley swirled her wine in her glass before taking a swig. "We saw Blaine just a few hours before we found her body. This man was with her during that time. I find it hard to believe that a hired gun could get her away from this Marc character and kill her in that three- or four-hour block of time. It is more likely that Marc killed her. We have to find him."

Max took a sip of his wine, a Sangiovese this time. "I don't disagree, but where do we start looking for him?"

"We need to find out more about him. We can start from the assumption that he and Blaine were staying somewhere in that little village. Maybe we go back there and ask around again, but with his picture, not hers."

"I doubt people are going to talk, especially if he's known around there."

"You're probably right. I also doubt that he is going to stick around there, given everything that is happening. So, if he moves, where would he move to?"

"Something makes me think that he or his family is from around here. You don't just pick out a small town and find a flat without some knowledge of the place or a connection to it." Max summoned a waiter while he was talking and silently ordered a plate of cheeses and meats by pointing to the same at the next table over.

"You hungry again, babe?" Finley asked. "We can order real dinner if you'd like."

"I'm fine with grazing for now, unless you want something more."

Finley shook her head. "I don't have much of an appetite right now. My brain and my stomach are a tumbled mess."

"Where is Evans when we need him? He would have the sort of information we need. How did Marc get involved with both Grant and Blaine? Is Marc Italian, and if so, from where? What was the significance of Assisi in all of this?"

"That's right! Blaine had an obsession with Assisi. Was it because of Marc or some other reason? We need more information."

Max pulled Finley closer to him and planted a kiss on her forehead. "He'll contact us soon. In the meantime, let's take our minds off the situation for a few minutes and try not to over-think things."

Finley nodded and settled into his arms.

By the next morning, Evans still hadn't called. He had said he needed a couple of days, but Finley was impatient doing nothing. Yet there wasn't much she could do until they had the information they needed to decide where to start looking for Marc. They had confirmed the previous night over drinks that the key to under-standing all that had happened, including Blaine's death, lay with finding Marc.

Sofia and Chuck were up and on the terrace when Max and Finley came downstairs. Unlike other mornings that had seen them rushing out to go to the police station or on sightseeing outings, this morning was a lazy one. Breakfast was laid out and coffee made. Sofia and Chuck also seemed to be operating at a more relaxed pace.

"Morning. Got big plans for the day?" Chuck asked, coffee cup in hand.

"Nope. Nothing in particular. We have hit a dead end, it seems," Max said over his shoulder as he filled a plate with bread and cheese. Sofia had gone into the kitchen to make him his eggs.

"Find out anything interesting from your talk with Grant? You seemed pretty anxious to confirm or extract something from him when you dropped us off."

Max dropped into the seat beside Finley and gave her a look of encouragement. She took a gulp of coffee before she spoke. "My suspicion was correct. I had a nagging feeling about the relation-ship between those three—Grant, his wife, and the man in the picture. The painting in the museum in Siena got me thinking. And Grant confirmed it last night."

"Confirmed what?" Chuck put down his cup and leaned forward.

"That the man in the picture, Marc, wasn't just Blaine's lover, he was also Grant's."

"Grant is gay, or at least bi," Max clarified.

Sofia walked back into the room with the eggs at just that moment. She stopped in her tracks and stared at Finley. "Grant is gay?"

Finley nodded. "I had no indication when we were married. I guess Grant denied that side of himself then. He didn't go into any detail about when his affair with Marc started. In fact, he didn't say much besides he didn't know Marc was Blaine's lover too."

"That explains his silence. I guess it took him a while to process that fact. He was betrayed twice." Sofia set the eggs in front of Max and gave Finley a sad smile. "Are you okay?"

Finley nodded again.

"I wonder if that was the reason his little wifey went crazy on him the last time. When she sliced him up and broke his ribs?" Chuck raised a brow and quirked his lips into a smirk.

"The affair—or should I say affairs, plural—were probably what started the argument, but I didn't get the impression that Blaine knew about Grant's preferences. Grant seems to have kept that well under wraps. I think she was under the assumption, like us, that there was another woman involved," Finley said.

"Agreed. That was a secret I think Grant was even hiding from himself," Max added.

"So now what? How does this change his defense?" Chuck asked.

Finley shrugged. "I don't really know. We're stumped."

"This boyfriend, Marc, is the key, I think. We need to find him. But we need more information from Evans so we can narrow down where to look for him," Max said.

"You think he's moved from San Giacomo where you saw him before?" Sofia asked.

"I would think so. Given the reaction we got from people when we were looking for Blaine, we are stuck until Evans gives us the information we need on this guy." Finley got up and poured herself more coffee. She held the pot up in offer. Max and Chuck accepted.

"Well, until Evans calls, how about we take a drive? Yesterday was good fun. You up for Trevi?" Chuck suggested.

"Sure. What's in Trevi?" Finley took her coffee back to the bench and sat down.

"It is a pretty, ancient little town on a hill that offers one of the best views in all of Umbria," Chuck said. "The trip up the hill is steep, but you can drive it. And then at the top of the hill, it's flat, so getting around is pretty easy."

"Sounds good. Let's do it." Max stood and gathered up the empty coffee cups and plates. "You driving, or am I?"

"I'll drive this time. The streets are just wide enough to fit the van."

"Maybe by the time we get back, Evans will have some information for us," Finley said.

During the drive to Trevi, the group avoided any mention of Grant or his predicament. There was little they could do beside rehash what had already been said. Instead, Chuck and Max kept Finley and Sofia entertained with stories from their gig days.

"Remember the wedding out in the pastureland of Pennsylvania?" Chuck's laugh came out as a snort. "Did I book that one, or did Jono?"

Max shook his head and shrugged. "I can't remember. Whoever did was smoking something. We thought it would be a couple of hours' drive since Pennsylvania is right across the bridge."

"Five hours later . . ." Chuck was laughing hard by now. "We had, like, ten minutes before we were supposed to play. And the father of the bride had made clear that if anything went wrong that ruined his little girl's special day, we wouldn't get paid."

"These guys were stripping out of their clothes in the back of the van while I was driving," Max said. "We pull up to this big, swanky country club. I open the rear doors, and they roll out, dressed to the nines in black tie and patent-leather shoes. It was like a scene from a movie."

"He grabs our gear, and we grab the instruments and walk in like it was all planned. Your boy Max was sweating bricks."

Max looked over his shoulder at Finley. "You know I was miserable, Fin. Sofia, I like getting places early. I hate to rush. That was the worst. Thank goodness we left early."

"It was supposed to be so we could eat before we played, but that never happened, so my stomach was growling all during the set." Chuck shook his head. "Papa tipped us well, so it was all good."

"You really were a roadie!" Finley squeezed Max's shoulder gently. "What other life experiences have you been keeping from me?"

"Nothing that matters, sweetheart." Max touched her hand. "Nothing that matters."

The town of Trevi was as Chuck had described it—a little jewel set into a hill. Founded by the Romans before the birth of Christ, the city had been an important commercial center between Florence and Rome.

"Trevi had one of the earliest printing presses in Italy, which helped the city flourish during the Renaissance," Sofia shared.

"You can see the wealth in some of the houses that are off the center road. Really big ones," Chuck added. "We'll walk around once we get to the top."

Chuck took his role as tour guide quite seriously. Once they had parked the car and unloaded his chair, he struck out on what ended up being a three-hour tour of several medieval churches, many with frescoed walls depicting scenes from the Bible.

"The fresco in the Church of the Madonna is probably one of the most famous. I'm not up on my Bible, but I think it is of the three kings and Jesus as a baby," Chuck said before suggesting that Max and Finley take peek inside.

What they saw was a richly colored depiction of the visit of the three kings after the birth of Jesus painted by Pietro Perugino, a well-known Renaissance artist of the Umbrian school who was the teacher of Raphael. The fresco had survived far better than many of the others Chuck had shown them, which were cracked and faded with time.

"This one has been painstakingly restored, and it shows. I wish more money could be donated to preserve these brilliant works of art," Sofia added. "But most will fall into complete disrepair, and the public will never see them."

When the tour was over, Chuck led them down an alleyway into the courtyard of what looked to be an old manor house. The facade of traditional stone was accentuated by an arched entryway flanked by twin towers. The courtyard itself was dotted with tables set for outdoor dining nestled among pots of olive and lemon trees.

"This region is known for its olive oil, and I think this place is the best for highlighting the allure of the olive." Chuck spoke the last words in tones that evoked mystery and seduction.

"Outside or in today, Signore Hammond?" a man, who Finley assumed was the owner, greeted them.

"You guys okay being outside? They can handle my chair inside, but it's such a lovely day," Chuck said.

The rest of the group agreed. The day had turned out to be glorious—bright, clear skies with only a passing cloud accompanied by a light breeze that cooled the heat of the midday sun. The table they occupied offered the best of the day's weather—sheltered sun that caught the cooling winds.

"This place is darling. How did you find it?" Finley asked when they were seated.

"Just one day when we were wandering. There are quite a few very good restaurants in town. The fare can be pretty basic in some, but the preparation is masterful," Chuck said. "This find was just a stroke of good luck. And the fact we can sit inside at times is a real plus."

"Can we turn the menu over to you? Finley and I eat anything, and you know our drink preferences," Max suggested. Finley nodded her agreement.

"Well, actually, I'm going to defer to my wife. She knows the foods and wines of this region better than any James Beard critic. As importantly, she know what to order when during the year," Chuck said.

Sofia blushed. "You exaggerate, Chuck. I just follow the seasons, and thus far, I haven't gone too wrong."

When the gentleman came back, Sofia made introductions all around. "This is Maximo, the owner of this little gem. He says he has lovely lamb chops and as a starter, stuffed zucchini blossoms. Do we all like lamb?"

Having secured agreement all around, Sofia launched into a conversation in Italian with Maximo on the lunch selections. When they finished, she handed Chuck the wine card. "We are having the zucchini blossoms and a pasta—I let him surprise us—followed by the baby lamb chops, so you need to find wines that work."

"Brilliantly done, my dear. I'm salivating already." Chuck smiled at his wife before calling Maximo over. After another consultation in Italian, he passed Maximo the wine list and leaned back in his chair. "I think we will dine very well this afternoon!"

They had just finished the main course when Finley's phone vibrated. She ignored the first few rings. But when she glanced down on the third ring, she excused herself and retired to the end of the courtyard.

"Evans, thank goodness."

"Hello. Sorry I kept you waiting so long, but it couldn't be helped," Evans hurried on. "I only have a couple of minutes, but I sent you a summary of what I found. The man is Marco, or Marc, Santori. He is a fund manager in Manhattan, pretty well-known. He and Grant may have known each other at Morgan Stanley, since they both worked there. Look, I have to run, but I hope this helps. Call if you need more."

With that, he was gone. Finley exhaled heavily and scrolled through her email for Evans's message. She pulled it up as she headed back to the table.

"Sorry about that, but it was Evans. I didn't know when he would get a chance to call again," Finley explained as she took her seat.

"What did he say about Marc?" Max took a long sip of his wine, another Sangiovese but this time melded with merlot.

"I'm reading his report now. He didn't have a lot of time to talk." Finley's eyes ran over the bulleted highlights Evans had compiled.

"Marc, or Marco, as he is sometimes known, is Italian but has lived most of his adult life in New York. Both he and Grant worked at Morgan Stanley, so they may have known each other for a couple of decades." Finley looked up and smirked. "I was right. He does speak English."

"Did they say where in Italy his family is from?" Max asked. "That's what we need right now. A starting place."

Finley ran her finger down the text on her screen. "Let me see . . . He's from Assisi, or at least a little town outside. That's why the fixation on Assisi. Blaine must have planned to meet him there."

"But how did she plan to get rid of her husband? She was traveling with him. Were they just going to run off, or were they going to kill him at some point? This is getting pretty sordid." Sofia frowned as she thought through the implications of what she was asking.

"I know. They must have been planning this for a while. Poor Grant." Finley sighed.

"Yes, but this still doesn't offer anything to change the police theory that this was a murder for hire by Grant. In fact, this strengthens that theory." Max leaned forward to make his point. "Grant found out about the betrayal by his wife and decided to put an end to it—by killing her."

"That his lover was involved was just ancillary. In fact, now he has a motive for blaming Marc for the murder. He would kill two betraying birds with one stone if Marc gets accused of murdering her," Chuck added.

"But you are forgetting that he didn't know about Marc being Blaine's lover until a couple of days ago. And he's kept quiet about knowing Marc. He hasn't implicated Marc at all. Rather, he seems to be protecting him." Finley let out a giant puff of air and sighed deeply. "We're going around in circles. We have to find Marc. He's the only one who can help us make sense of this."

15

N O SOONER HAD THEY ENTERED the house than Max and Finley were preparing to leave again. They were determined to leave no stone unturned in the search for Marc. On the way back from Trevi, Max and Chuck had mapped out towns and villages in the area that were off the beaten path and might be a good place for Marc to hide out.

On the outside chance that he was still there, they had driven through San Giacomo, the town where Finley had first spotted Blaine and Marc. The picture of Blaine's pretty face was still up in the tiny grocery store but had been taken down in the dress shop and the post office. They decided against posting pictures of Marc. That only would scare him into deeper hiding.

"I would suggest you start with Silvignano and then head to Grotti and Santa Croce. They're close together, so a little less driving. I would leave Pompagnano till last," Chuck recommended. "It's bigger, but it's on the other side of Spoleto. In each of these towns, everything revolves around the square. If you hit three or four places near the square, the word will spread."

"Today is the farmers market in Grotti, so the shops and stalls will be open later," Sofia added, pulling the day's purchases into the main hall. "If you get a chance, can you pick up a few more lemons and oranges? I was going to make another batch of sangria this evening."

Finley nodded and picked up the wicker shopping basket that hung on the hook near the kitchen door. "See you in a bit. Text me if there is anything else you need."

"We'll have a light dinner, if that is okay with you," Sofia said as she rolled Chuck out onto the terrace.

"More than okay. I will have gained quite a few pounds on this trip," Max said with a moan. "But lunch today was worth every bite."

Outside, the sun was still fairly high. The cafés and shops in even the smallest of towns were taking advantage of the warm weather. As expected, all but a few establishments in Santa Croce were bustling when Max and Finley drove in.

Max parked the car while Finley grabbed a handful of flyers from the back seat and stuffed them into her satchel. A few of the cafés around the plaza had thrown open the folding doors that faced the square and added extra outdoor tables that now spilled into the walkway. No one seemed to care. They were enjoying the afternoon.

"Shall we wander around this main area and maybe talk to a few of the restaurant owners?" Max asked as they started toward the main square.

"You mean you'll talk to the owners. I'll tag along." She tucked her arm into his to make the point clear.

The proprietors of the first few places shook their heads when Max showed them the picture of Marc, even after Max stressed that the man wasn't in trouble—a lie, but given the reaction they'd faced when looking for Blaine, they were taking no chances. There wouldn't be time for a do-over.

Finley was ready to give up and suggest that they move on to the next town. Max, however, liked the look of the little trattoria that was next and approached the owner before she could stop him.

When the owner saw the picture Max was holding, he nodded, tapping the flyer with his finger.

"Him? That's Marco. He was just here. He comes in every now and then for his coffee or a beer." He was looking around as he spoke, searching the square for Marc. In an instance, he saw him, and before Max or Finley could stop him, he called out, "Marco! Oy! Marco! These people are looking for you!"

Marc turned at the sound of his name, his hand halfway up in a friendly greeting. But when he saw Finley standing in the entrance to the restaurant, his smile faded. He hurriedly slipped into a nearby alley and was gone.

"In a hurry to get home. Guess he didn't want to talk!" the owner said with a shrug before heading back into the restaurant to look after the bar.

"Damn!" Max slammed his hand against the back of a nearby chair when the man left. "So close. But at least we know he's still around."

"And that this is home—for now. So what do we do next?" Finley kept her eyes on the side of the plaza where Marco had been. "He's either going to move again or lie low for a few days, hoping we'll give up."

Max cursed in disappointment under his breath, but he had to agree. "Let's go to Grotti, get the groceries, and then go home. That's it for tonight, I guess."

"And maybe for the next few days." She touched his arm. "We'll find him again. I know we will. Don't worry."

"You'd have thought Grant was *my* friend, not yours, the way I'm reacting! But I want justice for that poor woman. She might have been crazy, but she didn't deserve to die. And Grant deserves his kids back."

Knowing there was little point in searching for Marc over the next several days, Finley decided to head into Spoleto the next morning to take some pictures. She had been so caught up in helping Grant build a defense that she had seen few of the sights she had marked in her guidebook on the flight over.

"I think I'll start at the art museum and wander around to the theater. Then I might walk up to the convent. The stones and the light should make for some nice shots," she said. "I may even stop in for the last part of Mass at the cathedral. We'll see. Please don't hold lunch up for me."

"Well, you have good weather again, at least," Chuck observed, coffee in hand, surveying the panoramic countryside in front of him. He glanced over at Max, who was his mirror image, eyes scanning the olive- and hay-colored hills and valleys. "You going with her?"

Max shook his head. "I only get in the way,"

Finley protested. "That's not true. You help."

"How?" Max turned to look up at her and smiled. The quarter angle of her face as she reached for the jam on the sideboard caught the light, and he followed the tilted slope of her eyes, the rise of her cheekbone, the curve of her lips as he waited for her reply.

"You point out interesting subjects, hold my equipment, and help me set up shots."

"Uh-huh," Max teased. "But mostly, I hear, 'Sweetheart, would you mind stepping out of my frame?'"

Finley shrugged as she took her seat. "Well, yes, there's some of that. But that's only sometimes."

Max chuckled. "So, in answer to your question, Chuck, no, I will not be going. I'll stick around here with you and Sofia, if that's okay. We haven't had much of a chance to catch up. Grant seems to have grabbed the center of attention most of the time. "

Sofia made the rounds with a coffeepot in hand. "We'd love to have your company, you know. Maybe Chuck will feel like playing later, and you can record some of it."

"Woman, this crap doesn't need to be recorded," Chuck argued. "What for?"

Sofia kissed his forehead and refilled his cup. "For me."

Finley left Max and Sofia to squabble with Chuck about the recording of his guitar playing. She understood his concern, but she knew, as did Sofia, that ALS would soon rob him of the ability to play at all, and his beautiful music would be silenced forever.

She took advantage of the glorious weather to push the sunroof all the way back on the short drive into Spoleto. The sun, coupled with the sandy flats and sage-colored hills, brought back memories of trips through the wine country of California. The tang of rosemary and dust hit her nostrils as the wind brushed against her face.

"This is the life," she muttered to herself as she tooled down the road. "Maybe I could get used to a slower pace."

She lowered the volume on the radio as she entered the city proper. The neighborhood vacillated street by street between nearly deserted in the main commercial areas and dotted with pedestrians in the residential. She parked the little car in the Lidl parking lot and made her way toward her first stop, the Palazzo Collicola Galleria d'Arte Moderna.

Even though the museum itself was closed, the outside environs were sufficiently interesting, especially given the play of light on the building's curvature. She took a few frames at different angles before deciding to move on. The plan was to walk to San Ponziano before curving back to the cathedral. If she timed it right, she could catch the last third of Mass.

Then, take a few shots of the nave before finding a nice little place for lunch. She was looking forward to pasta at whatever trattoria she stumbled upon. She would linger over a glass of wine, soak up a bit more sun, and then head back. A leisurely plan for a lazy Sunday.

The walk to San Ponziano took longer than she had planned, so while the architecture begged her to slow down and take it in, her desire to sit in on even a little bit of Mass pulled her toward the cathedral. She paused several times to snap candid shots of children playing in the fountains and shawled grandmas kibbitzing at the corners, the hallmarks of everyday life that she loved to capture on film.

In one small street, she stopped to carefully compose a shot of a dapper man on his way to church—or an assignation—against the background of an ancient tower. The crisp whiteness of his linen suit and Panama hat against the dusty brown of the building with its rust-tiled roof offered an interesting contrast.

"I'm going to like that one, I know." She hurried on without even checking the frame, talking to herself as she navigated the cobbled streets. "Don't want to miss Mass."

When she reached the cathedral, she slipped through one of the open doors at the back and quietly found a pew. People were lining up for Communion. She contemplated joining them but decided against it. It had been a long time since she had taken Communion, and even longer since she had been to confession. Things were dodgy enough with Grant's situation. *It's best not to get on God's bad side.*

She followed the rest of the order of service, singing along to the hymns that had been part of her childhood. She waited afterward, until most of the parishioners had left, before she pulled out her camera and discreetly took a series of pictures of the vividly detailed frescoes above the altar. The bright sunlight illuminated the vibrant greens, blues, and reds of the paintings, whose gold highlights caught the rays and tossed them back in flashes of blinding white.

It had taken several adjustments of the settings to capture the full glory of the frescoes' play of light, but after several minutes, Finley smiled broadly at the shots as she scrolled through what she had captured on film. She put the cap back on her lens and dropped the camera into her satchel. As she strolled up the center aisle, two young priests greeted her with slight bows and welcoming smiles, heading to the area behind the altar.

A spear of light blinded her for a moment when she reached the door, and she stood looking about until her eyes adjusted. Now in the courtyard, she turned sharply to walk past the cathedral toward lunch but instead ran headlong into a man in a white T-shirt.

"So sorry. Clumsy of me. *Scusi!*" Finley babbled, briefly glancing up.

His face was haloed by the sun, blocking out his features. Finley had expected him to step aside, but instead, he stood firm. Finley stepped to the right to go around him, but he matched her step to block her way. Instinctively, she clutched her satchel to her when he addressed her in unaccented English.

"Keep your voice down, and play along."

She raised her head to look into his eyes, but the sun thwarted her. "Marc?"

"I don't know who you are or how you know my name, but for now, you're coming with me." He pushed something into the small of her back and guided her around to the side of the church.

"You don't have to do this," Finley said softly. "We just had some questions."

"I'll ask the questions now. You'll just shut up. Unless you have a death wish!" he said with a hiss.

Finley did as he said. He slipped his arm through hers on one side as he pressed the object into her back.

"We're going to take a little ride."

Finley considered elbowing him and running, but the coldness of the object digging into her spine made her reconsider. *Where are those priests now? Probably finishing up the wine in the sacristy instead battling the bad guys!* she thought testily.

As they rounded the corner, he shoved her toward a car parked in the alleyway. She stumbled, and he took advantage, slipping a burlap shopping bag over her head and quickly drawing the string. "Get in, and don't even try to scream. It'll be life limiting."

Once she was in the back of the car, he pulled ropes out from under the seat and bound her hands and feet. He then jumped into the front seat and screeched down the alley. The quick movement threw her sideways across the seat, and she struggled not to fall onto the floor.

One of the benefits of small cars. Less room to tumble.

Having no knowledge of the terrain, Finley stopped trying to figure where they were going and focused instead on what she was going to do once they got there. The weight of her satchel still wrapped around her arm dragged her forward at an awkward angle so that she heard her phone fall to the floor of the car. Marc made no comment; she assumed he didn't hear it fall.

She could see through the fabric of the bag that the screen had lit up, enabling her to find it. Getting it, however, was going to be a different matter. As much as Max complained about her habit of always keeping her phone on vibrate, which resulted in a raft of missed calls, she was glad now that she didn't have to worry about it ringing while she gyrated her body to retrieve it.

After several tries, she managed to flip over so she was facing the seat back. Using her feet to move the phone toward her, she managed to position her hands just above the phone. As she leaned back to grab it, the car halted suddenly with a jerk that tossed her to the floor.

"What the hell?" Marc quickly stopped the car and came around to push her upright.

In the time that it took for him to walk around the car to the side with her head, Finley had palmed the phone and pushed it into the back of her jeans.

"Thought you were going to catch me off guard and kick me with your feet, but I outsmarted you." He grabbed her shoulders and pushed her upright. "Sit up and stay up!"

She jerked her shirt down firmly over the back of her pants as he heaved her back onto the seat. "It's hard with my hands tied. You try it."

"Don't be a smart-mouth. Just shut up."

They drove several minutes more before they entered a village, judging from the street sounds she heard. She wondered whether it was the same one she and Max had wandered through the previous evening. Marc slowed the car, and Finley could hear the loud noises of people talking and dishes and glasses clanking before the noise grew distant. The sounds grew quiet, and Marc stopped the car, then pulled her out onto the street, the gun still digging into her back.

"We're going to have a nice little chat," Marc mumbled under his breath as he pulled her into a building and pushed her along a hallway.

She could hear the sounds of children playing, pots scraping, men talking. She tried to count the number of doors on one side based on the rise and fall of noises as she passed.

At what felt like the end of the hallway, Marc stopped. She heard keys rattle, a lock tumble, and the door push open.

Despite his prodding her with the gun, she paused before she entering. *Six doors on my left as I go past. The plaza is to my right when I come out of the door*, she noted. *In case I decide to run.*

Inside, Marc led her over to a table and roughly jammed her into a chair, hitting her hip bone in the process.

"Ow!" she cried, pulling herself back from the table as she sat.

"Are you going to say I beat you too?" Marc shouted, untying the cord on the bag and snatching it off her head.

He was more handsome than she recalled from their first encounter. Dark curly hair that he tucked behind his ears when he took off his flat cap. A broad, muscular chest and well-built arms. A marked contrast to Grant's athletic lankiness, but she could see what Blaine might have seen in him. Large pools of warm, almost puppyish brown eyes and a dimpled chin. She could see, too, what comfort Grant might have sought there.

Marc pulled up a chair so he was facing her directly.

"Look, I don't want hurt you." He took in a deep breath and huffed it out. "I don't want to hurt anyone. I just want you and your boyfriend or husband or whatever he is to stop following me. And that gigolo too!"

Finley shook her head and shrugged. "I don't know what you're talking about. My husband and I just wanted to ask you some questions."

Marc jumped up and ran into the kitchen. She heard him rummaging around in the drawers and slamming cabinet doors before coming out with a roll of duct tape.

"No questions. You're going to listen! Not talk!" he screamed, looming over her and turning the roll of tape around in his hand.

"I'm listening," Finley said softly.

"I need you to get your husband to tell the police to back off. To leave me alone. I need to figure things out. It's all gone wrong!"

"But the police aren't looking—"

"Lies! All lies! There are plainclothes cops all over the place. Following me. Spying on me." Marc was pulling at his hair, which now fell over his face, making him look maniacal.

"Who is spying on you? The police—"

"Shut up! Just shut up!" He began pacing in circles, huffing and puffing as he walked. "That wasn't the plan. It all went wrong."

"Marc, what happened? Tell me—"

He crossed the narrow room in two strides. She drew back in fear as he tore off two large pieces of tape and plastered them across her mouth.

"Now you're going to listen! You're going to shut up and listen!"

16

MARC DROPPED BACK DOWN INTO the chair, his head in his hands. "It wasn't supposed to go like this. All I wanted was for Grant to get jealous . . . and come back to me."

Finley's eyebrows arched to her hairline. *This wasn't a threesome. This was lover's revenge!*

The man's plaintive tale sounded like something from a Harlequin novel. "I just wanted him back, but he said he wanted her. So, to make him jealous, I took her as mine instead. She was looking for an adventure, and I promised her one."

He continued, his voice distant even though he was right in front of her. "All she had to do was get to Assisi. When he decided not to make the side trip, she was supposed to jump off the train and come to me, and then we were supposed to go away for a while together. It was that simple.

"I knew she would get tired of me. Grant would get tired of her antics, and he would come back. It would be like it was before. It was so simple."

Finley grunted her question instinctively, not paying attention to the tape sealing her mouth shut.

Marc intuited the question and, with a sad smile, answered it. "And then she had to go crazy on me. She was kicking and screaming. Cursing like a mother!"

Finley's eyes softened, urging him to go on, even though she knew what had happened.

"I didn't mean to hurt her. I just wanted her to stop hitting and kicking me. I pushed her away, and she fell. She didn't move. She just didn't move." He closed his eyes and whispered the last words almost like a prayer before opening them and looking sadly at Finley. "I didn't mean to hurt her."

They were both silent for several minutes, Marc staring vacantly at his feet, Finley looking at him. *There are a couple of ways this could turn out,* she thought. *He could ask for my help in turning himself in, or he could leave me tied up and make a run for it.* Then she considered a third. *Or he could figure, 'In for a penny, in for a pound,' and kill me too.*

Marc rose suddenly and went into the kitchen. She heard the refrigerator open and then several drawers and cabinets slam. After a while, he came out and laid a bulging nylon drawstring on table. He turned immediately and headed toward the back of the tiny apartment. She could hear drawers opening and closing, heavy objects being moved around, and finally, the zip of a bag.

He marched back into the room and snatched the tape off her mouth. "What's his number?"

"Whose?" Finley mumbled, touching her tape-scorched lips gently with her tongue and shaking off the pain.

"Your husband's! He's going to call the police and tell them to give me twelve hours to get out of the country, or he's never going to see his cute little wife again."

"I told you—"

"I don't care what you say. The police are going to back off, or else!" He held his phone up and waited.

"Do you have WhatsApp? It might be easier and less likely to be traced." Finley didn't know if that was true or not, but Max was more likely to answer a call to his London WhatsApp than a random local number. And she wanted to be sure he picked up.

"What's his WhatsApp, then?"

"Plus forty-four . . ." She rattled off the remaining numbers and waited. Now she knew how Grant must have felt, dialing her number and praying someone would pick up. After the fourth ring, Finley held her breath. *Please pick up! Please!*

"'Lo?"

"You're going to do as I say," Marc started.

"Who is this?" Max said angrily.

"Max!" Finley cried out, her voice cracking. "Don't hang up!"

"Finley! Sweetheart, where are you?"

"With Marc—"

"Yeah, she's with me. So you are going to listen to me and do exactly what I say. Understand?"

"Where are you? What have you done to her? This—"

"I said shut up and listen! I am not going to jail for this! I didn't do anything but shove her. She's the one who attacked me, and now *I'm* going to have to pay? *Like hell!*"

Marc was now screaming into the phone and starting to pace again. Finley knew she needed to calm him down, or Max's repetition of the same message—the police don't care—was not going to go over well.

"Marc, Max is listening. He'll stop talking and listen if you'll stop screaming. You don't want the neighbors to call the police, do you?" Finley cooed. "If not, you need to tell Max what you want in a calm voice."

Marc seemed to have gotten the message. The pacing slowed, and he spoke in a normal tone. "I want you to get on the phone with the police and tell them to give me a chance to get out of the city. Tell them to call off the plainclothes guys they have following me."

"What guys, Marc? Can you describe them?"

Finley knew Max would have no idea what Marc was talking about, and his questioning might spark another round of ranting.

"They know them! You know them too! You must. Wherever you go, they go too. That boxer, bruiser-looking dude with the broken nose and cauliflower ears. And then the dandy, Mr. *GQ*." Marc walked to other side of the room and hissed. "You call them off—*now!*"

Finley could feel the growing weight of Max's response, how he had taken his time to choose his words carefully.

"Marc, I want you to hear me out before you jump down my throat. You want time to get away, and I want my wife back. So please listen."

Marc got ready to go into a tirade again, but Finley held his eyes and begged him wordlessly to listen to Max's proposition.

"Go ahead, Max," she said.

Max took a breath. "The police have their man. They have Grant. They aren't looking for you."

"But Grant didn't do it. I can't let him hang for something I did," Marc implored. "You have to tell them I did it, but they have to give me time."

"May I propose another option, then, that helps both of you?" Max offered, his voice almost encouraging.

Marc slumped down in the chair in front of Finley again and put the phone on the table, the gun in his other hand. For a moment, he looked like a man defeated, faced with saving himself or saving his lover. "What do you propose?"

"That you write a note confessing and leave it—and Finley— wherever you are. That will get Grant off. And then you just leave. Drive or fly wherever you want to go. We won't 'find' that letter until tomorrow, and by then, you'll be long gone." Max modulated his voice so that he sounded like he was promoting vacation travel instead of negotiating Finley's release.

"I like that idea, but I have a variant." Marc had come back alive, not ranting but posturing. He squinted his eyes at Finley and gave a smirking half laugh. "I'll write the letter, but I'm taking the lady as insurance that I have time to get out of the coun—"

Max broke in, his voice ragged with anger. "Unless you release my wife, no deal."

"Max. Max, it's okay. Why don't you and Evans just wait there while Marc writes the letter? And then maybe when we get to Croatia or Malta or even Corsica tomorrow, he'll call you and let you know where he left me?" Finley turned to look at Marc, who was pulling paper from a nearby desk. He had put down the gun, but it was still within his reach. "And thank you for putting down the gun."

She heard Max gasp at the mention of a gun. She continued. "Max, can you and Evans do that for me? Marc is writing the letter as we speak."

Marc looked up from the paper. He had moved the gun closer to him. "I like that proposition. I don't want to hurt her. I just want to get away. I'll write the letter. We'll head out, and I'll let you know tomorrow where to find her."

He clicked off before Max could reply.

Finley waited until he had finished his letter before she spoke. "Max will keep his word. You need to keep yours."

As he sealed the envelope, Marc replied with a sneer that could have had any number of meanings. "Of course. I don't want anyone else to get hurt. But we need to get out of here now, just in case."

Chuck and Sofia had heard much of the phone exchange.

"What are you going to do?" Chuck asked. "He sounds pretty erratic."

"Thank goodness Finley sounded calm." Sofia moved from the bench closer to Chuck. "Tell me, what do you need us to do?"

"If you can get me some paper and a pen, that would help." Max picked up his phone and prepared to dial. "And as to Finley, this isn't her first rodeo. That woman and her sister get into more scrapes than you could imagine. The fact that she asked for Evans means this one is trickier than the others."

He had almost punched in the number for Evans that he remembered from Finley's mobile when the phone in his hand rang.

"Max? This is Vittorio."

Max had no idea who the man with the heavy Italian accent was, although he seemed quite familiar with Max. "Who is this?"

"Vittorio, a friend of Evans. We have been keeping eyes on you. I know where your wife is, but we need the police to move in to help. The man who is holding her has a gun."

"I know. I just talked to her, and she alerted me. He's ready to move her now. We don't have time for the police. Where are you? Can you see her? Is she okay? He's crazy."

Vittorio sighed. "I have a man on her. Have for a few days. Evans was concerned. My man saw her taken, but when he saw the gun, he backed off. Just followed her. He doesn't have eyes on her now, but he knows where they are."

"Is your man armed?"

"What you think?" Vittorio scoffed. "*Naturalmente!* Look. I come pick you up. We talk about what to do on the way."

"What do I do in the meantime? Shall I get Evans in on this?" Max asked as he moved around the room, packing his day sack.

"He's already aware. I call him. Your wife, she smart. Her phone is on, and Evans put a trace on it. So, if they move, and Mafaldo lose them, we still find them!"

Max chuckled. "Leave it to Fin to save herself. Yeah. Come get me. I'll send you—"

"No need. I know where you are. I will be there in four minutes, according to the GPS. Three, based on my driving."

Before he could hang up, Max heard a car on the road.

"What can we do?" Chuck demanded. "We know people who might be able to help."

"Right now, just stay put in case Finley manages to get away and needs a lift. I'll call the police, but I know what they're going to say. I'm going to have to trust Evans with this. Finley does!"

The man in the slate-gray Alfa Romeo Giulia could have modeled for *Vogue Italia*. He didn't stop to get out but rather swung the passenger door open so Max could jump in. In seconds, they were off again.

"Max, pleasure to meet you. Although I would have preferred a less dangerous introduction. But we manage."

Max had to laugh at the man's offhanded gentility. Finley would like him. "I agree, but once this is over, we can trade stories over a bottle of wine."

"*Accordo!* Mafaldo is still in Santa Croce, where he is holding her."

"We were just there last night!" Max sighed. "Finley thought he would hole up for a few days before he moved again. Something must have spooked him. No matter. We know where he is."

"I say to Mafaldo to hang back, so he not see him." Vittorio chuckled as he shifted to a higher gear and skimmed over the roadway. "He is always ready for a fight. This time, I tell him, no fight."

"Thanks for that. Last thing we want is Marc scared into thinking he has to shoot his way out, and Finley getting caught in the crossfire."

Vittorio gave Max a side-glance. "Your wife, she will be safe."

Vittorio pulled into an open space not far from the square and cut the engine. He leisurely slid out of the car and reached into the back seat to retrieve his hat. He felt around on the floor of the back seat before pulling out a solid ebony walking stick with a carved silver handle.

He shrugged as he donned his hat, adjusted the lapels of his cream linen suit, and held up the stick. "You never know when it can come in handy."

He sauntered across the square, greeting café diners as he went while Max tried to hurry the pace. *This is not a Sunday stroll. Step it up, man!* At the far end of the square, Vittorio halted and stuck his head around the corner of a narrow street before leading Max down the alleyway. He stopped again at the middle of the block and entered an apartment building slowly. Silently, almost catlike, he walked to the end of the hall.

The door was half-open. Vittorio paused and put his finger to his lips before using his cane to push the door back on its hinges. He waited and listened, his eyes darting from side to side. He felt his phone vibrate in his pocket. He pulled it from his jacket and looked at the screen.

"All clear. Mafaldo! You can come out," Vittorio announced as he strode confidently into the apartment.

"Torio—" Mafaldo started through the door, but Finley darted around him and into Max's arms.

"Max!" She buried her head in his shoulder as he enveloped her.

"Crazy girl! What did you get yourself into this time?" he whispered into her hair. He pulled her back and looked her over before gently kissing her eyelids. "Are you okay? He didn't hurt you, did he?"

"No, he was scared. And scared people do stupid things, but he didn't hurt me." Finley relaxed in his arms. "He got away, but not before he wrote a confession."

"Your lady, she grab it from the table while I try to get her to hide," Mafaldo said. "I don't know if he comes back or not. He see me in the hall and then run."

Finley filled in the rest of the details. "Marc taped my mouth again and went to put his things in the car. I guess he was going to come get me once he loaded up. While he was gone, Aldo somehow got past him and entered the apartment. Marc must have seen him when he came back in and bolted. I was afraid if he did come back, he might grab the confession and run."

Vittorio nodded at Finley while catching Max's eye. "I told you, she very smart."

"Let's get you out of here and home safe." Max put his arm around Finley's waist to guide her out into the hall, but she had other ideas.

She spun around and stood in the center of the tiny room. "We need to search this place thoroughly before we leave. If he does come back, he'll make away with every bit of evidence, even proof of Blaine's existence!"

"Finley, you're in shock. You need rest. Let the police or these guys do it," Max begged, motioning to Vittorio and Mafaldo.

Vittorio smiled and touched Finley's cheek avuncularly. "He is right. The adrenaline will leave, and you will fall like rock. Go to the car and wait. Mafaldo and I, we do good look, and then we leave. Okay?"

Finley agreed and picked up her satchel. She pulled a small envelope from her bra and placed it inside the pocket of her bag. "The confession. We don't want to lose that."

Seated in the car, the fatigue overtook her, just as Max had expected. She leaned her head against his shoulder and listened to the lullaby of his breathing.

"You want to tell me what happened?" he asked quietly.

"Yeah. I know I'm going to have to repeat it a few times, but I want to tell you first." Finley leaned up and kissed the line of his jaw. "I was scared he would take me away from you for a long time. I stopped thinking he was going to kill me. He just wanted to get away. It was an accident."

"Start from the beginning."

"I followed my photo plan, just like I told you before I headed out." Finley pulled out her camera as she recounted the events of the morning. She stopped periodically to show him shots she'd taken along the way. "He intercepted me just after Mass. Before lunch."

As if on cue, her stomach growled.

"We'll get you food as soon as we get home. A nice glass of sangria and some dinner," Max promised, ruffling her hair. "Sofia is like your mother. When she's nervous, she cooks. So Sofia has been cooking—a lot. There will be more than enough to eat!"

17

T took less than fifteen minutes for Vittorio and Mafaldo to search that little apartment. When they reached the car, Mafaldo's black shirt and jeans were covered in dust. Vittorio's suit was still immaculate.

"There was nothing. He took everything that was his and left. Funny. We find nothing of the lady," Vittoria relayed.

"He must have removed anything earlier. He's had a few days since we found her," Max considered. "Now, to figure out his next move."

"Well, I know what my next step is going to be. A bath, then food, then sleep," Finley shared.

"I think I would reorder that. Sofia said dinner is ready and to hurry home," Max said. "She's invited you two to join us. No doubt Chuck wants the real story!"

Vittorio had them back at the house in no time. Even as the car was rolling to a stop, Sofia had thrown open the door and hurried out, looking for Finley. Finding her in the back with Max, she flung open the door and covered Finley's face with kisses.

"You had me so worried!" she exclaimed. "Even Chuck, who weathers everything, was concerned. He will be glad to see you. Now, let's go in and eat."

While Sofia and Max got Vittorio and Mafaldo something to drink, Finley ran up to take a quick shower. She had just come out of the bathroom when Max entered the room.

"All clean?" He scanned her towel-wrapped body lovingly with his eyes. "No major scrapes or bruises?"

Finley shook her head. "Nope. Not even a hangnail. I told you, he just wanted to get away. There were a couple of times I wondered whether I had misread him—if he was more dangerous than I thought—but each time, something would make him crumble and focus on getting away."

"You were lucky, you know." He came over to her and kissed her wet hair.

"I know. But I didn't ask for it."

"You never do! But somehow, you and Whitt literally get yourselves into death-defying situations. When we have kids, what are you going to do?"

"Max, I swear I try to be careful. I didn't go looking for him. He found me." Finley searched his eyes. "When we have a family, I can't be wrapped in cotton wool, or whatever the Brits call our Bubble Wrap. I can't be afraid all the time of what might happen. What they have to see is that I—we—can deal with whatever comes."

"You really do insist on playing the hand all the way out." Max smiled, recalling Finley's frequent admonition to herself and her family not to let fear force them to fold but to courageously play the hand they were dealt to the end of the game.

Finley nodded. "Don't know any other way."

"Well, get dressed. Vittorio and—is it *Aldo* or *Mafaldo*?—are filling us in on their conversation with Evans."

"I'll hurry. I want to hear that," Finley said, pulling on a pair of black capris and a black long-sleeved T-shirt. "And it's either

Aldo or *Mafaldo*, although he apparently prefers *Aldo*. Says *Mafaldo* sounds like a creepy uncle."

Max chortled. "Have to agree with him there!"

"All done," Finley said as she ran a brush through her short hair and threw it on the bed. She checked her image in the mirror as she left the room.

He may like my hair long, but I couldn't have gotten dressed this quickly with it long. And after Jaipur . . . Her mind flashed back quickly to an incident not so long ago in India when a thief had used Finley's long hair as a weapon before she'd stomped on his foot and disarmed him. She had cut it again shortly thereafter.

Finley could hear Vittorio's elegant, melodious voice as she entered the room.

"What part are you on now?" she asked. "I need to get the full scoop."

"The writer in you!" Sofia commented. "Why don't we take a break and move to the table, so we can eat while our guests tell you the story?"

At the table, Vittorio and Mafaldo focused on filling their plates before continuing their story. Max hadn't exaggerated when he said Sofia had cooked up a storm. In addition to the local cheeses, bread, and dried meats that were always on the long board as starters, tonight Sofia had prepared a *ribollita*, a hearty Umbrian bean soup; *pappardelle alla lepre*, pasta with a meaty ragu; *pollo alla diavola*, a spiced chicken; a pork loin called *arista*; and a *panzanella*, or bread salad. Instead of serving it in courses, she laid it out family style. Finley assumed this was so that she didn't have to miss anything while she was in the kitchen.

"So let me recap while you eat," Chuck said. "They got a call from Evans. Must have been shortly after you guys spoke to him the last time. He called Vittorio, and Vittorio called Aldo here."

Aldo bowed in assent, his mouth full of the rich pasta.

"How do you know Evans, though? What made him call you?" Finley asked.

Vittorio responded with a nonchalant wave of his hand. "Evans and I go back long time. We work together from time to time. Mafaldo, he always works with me."

Finley and Max exchanged glances. They both knew the types of work that Evans did and assumed Vittorio must also work undercover.

"Let me finish the summary, or we'll be here all night!" Chuck groused. "So, Aldo was put to following you, Finley, while Vittorio covered Marc, Blaine, and anybody else they thought might be involved."

"That is correct," Vittorio said. "We see all your interactions with Marco. Sometimes we follow you. Sometimes we anticipate. Sometimes we intercept."

"What does that mean?" Max asked.

"We didn't expect you to go to Trevi, for example. We think you stay in, so I tell Mafaldo to go play golf."

Finley chuckled to herself at the mental image of the Hulk look-alike playing a round. But she kept her reaction in check.

"Was there a need to follow us on that trip?" Finley asked. "We had backed off, hadn't we?"

"What you didn't know was that we had put a trace on the car Marco was using, and he was in that area."

Sofia blanched. "Oh, goodness!"

"So, can't we use that trace to find him now?" Max was alert to the possibility that they might be able to track Marc and urge the police to apprehend him before he reached the border.

Vittorio answered, gently wiping his mouth on his napkin and giving an apologetic little shrug. "Unfortunately, the man changed cars. No time to attach the new bug."

"Then we're back to crossing our fingers and hoping we catch him before he leaves the country," Finley said. "Now back to your story, Chuck. Sorry to keep interrupting."

"Good questions, girl. No problem. So, he sent Aldo to play golf, and when he sees us head to Trevi, he jumps in his car for a nice sightseeing outing. He said there were a few times that we were within a couple of streets of him."

"At that time, I know you look for him, but we have no evidence he done anything wrong. I need that before I call police to arrest him," Vittorio said.

"And you still have nothing," Chuck declared, shaking his head and taking a gulp of his wine.

"I wouldn't say that, exactly." Finley pulled out her phone. "Sorry for bringing this to the dinner table, but we did get a confession from him. I opened it immediately after Aldo cut me loose and took a picture with my phone, just in case."

"Does he really confess?" Chuck asked. "But why? Why not put some BS in there and save his skin?"

"Because he was in love with Grant. Plain and simple. He didn't want to see him in prison for something that was an accident," Finley stated.

"Are you sure it was an accident?" Chuck looked skeptical.

Finley nodded. "He talked about Blaine in a tantrum, the same way Grant did. He tried to fend her off, and she fell. He didn't say much about what happened after that, and I didn't push. We knew what happened. That was enough."

"So, what does the confession say?" Chuck was curious.

Finley scrolled through her gallery until she found it. "'I, Marco Tomaso Santori, do swear that the death of Blaine Lambert was an accident. She was hitting and kicking me, so I pushed her, and she fell. She hit her head and stopped moving. I didn't mean to hurt her. Grant Lambert, her husband, had nothing to do with it. He was not in the room or even the city as far as I know. He deserves to be released. I took her to the well on the old Fuscati vineyard property and left her. I'm sorry. I didn't intend for any of this to happen, but I confess that it did.'"

"A rather rambling confession, but it does relay the facts," Max commented.

"He doesn't say anything about how he moved her or why he chose that well. Nothing." Chuck sounded disappointed. "He just said it was an accident."

"I don't think he was thinking as a lawyer but as a man who didn't want his lover to spend his life in prison for something he did," Finley concluded.

Everyone ate in silence for a few minutes as the impact of the confession sunk in.

"Signora Hammond, this is one of best meals I have in long time. *Mi nonna* make *la lepre*. So long ago. This so good!" Mafaldo announced as Sofia ladled more onto his plate.

"Another thing it doesn't cover is what happened to Blaine's things—her clothes and especially her jewelry." Finley leaned back in her seat as she pondered this. "Where did all that stuff go?"

"Marc must have taken them," Chuck said.

"Maybe, but the duffel he had was small, barely enough for a couple of changes of clothes. Max, you said the lady who owned the dress shop in the town they were staying in said she came in and bought a few outfits. So, where are they?"

"She did, but what jewelry are you talking about, sweetheart?" Max picked up his glass and savored the wine, his eyes fixed on Finley.

"The ones she had on in the pictures."

"You've got me confused now, girl. What jewelry?" Chuck asked. "I don't remember seeing anything in those photos."

Finley jumped up and retrieved her camera from her satchel in the hall. She sat down and scanned quickly through the frames until she reached the early pictures in San Giacomo of Blaine and Marc. She searched for the best one that showed her earrings, a necklace, and a bracelet.

"There! You see? I know Whitt could identify them better than I, but that is a Lalaounis Hercules Knot necklace, retails for about twenty-five thousand dollars. The matching bracelet is probably another ten thousand. The earrings are hard to see, but I think those are Hermès—about two thousand."

"May I see?" Vittorio asked, holding his hand out for the camera. He enlarged the image and nodded with a satisfied confirmation. "Your wife, she not only smart, she know jewelry. She is right. Very high-end jewels."

"And nothing was found on her body when they pulled her from the well. So, where did it go?" Finley looked around the group for an answer.

"Good catch, girl," Chuck muttered. "Solved the murder and spotted a robbery."

"You must call the police. You have a confession and have discovered something else they need to investigate," Sofia said.

"The problem is I think Marc took them and is going to use them to hightail it out of Dodge. It's too late to search for them tonight, but by morning, I bet he's going to bring them out of hiding. We need to be there," Finley asserted.

"At the rate the police have moved thus far, he'll have himself set up nicely in Thailand before the cops here even finish the initial police inquiry," Max postulated.

"Which means we have to find him," Finley announced.

"Sweetheart, easier said than done." Max touched her arm. "How do you propose we do that?"

Finley engaged each of the people around the table. "With a little bit of manpower—and a lot of luck."

18

EARLY THE NEXT MORNING, MAX and Finley were out and on their way
to Assardi's office. Based on their previous engagements with
the police, they were not hopeful that the confession would do
anything to advance Grant's cause. While Officer Manzo was
more willing to consider alternative theories, he indicated that he
had seen nothing to date that altered the police theory that Grant
had hired someone to do away with Blaine. Maybe the confession
would change that. They would leave it to Assardi to deliver it.

The attorney was in his office, enjoying a cappuccino when
they walked in. "Welcome! What brings you in today? Can I offer
you an espresso or cappuccino?"

"A kidnapping and a confession," Finley said matter-of-factly.
"And a *lungo*, if you don't mind."

Max placed his order for a *lungo* as well and watched as
Assardi's face clouded over.

"Please start over. Who was kidnapped, and who confessed
and to what?" He reached for his pad and pen, having placed the
coffee orders.

"Finley was kidnapped by Marc, the man who we repeatedly told the police needed to be found," Max recounted. "And during that abduction, she managed to secure a confession from him that exonerates Grant and solves Blaine's murder!"

Assardi stared at Finley, who was now quietly sipping her coffee. Her raised eyebrow suggested that Max's recounting of her saga had left her less than amused at the police handling of the case.

"Had the police followed our leads and brought Marc in for questioning, I likely would not have been taken at gunpoint and tied up. But the police, including Officer Manzo, have not been interested in finding out what actually happened but rather in writing some TV version of an investigation narrative," Finley said.

"Let me call Manzo now and see if we can get him over here." The lawyer picked up his landline and began dialing the number.

"If he is not available, we don't have time to wait around. Marc stole Blaine's jewelry, and unless we find him soon, he will leave the country with the jewelry and you'll never find him again," Max added.

"Marc needs to be caught, or the convoluted wheels of justice here will end up tossing the confession. Grant will still lose his children." Finley placed the cup back in the saucer and retrieved the envelope from her satchel. "Here is the confession. I took pictures again, just in case."

Assardi sighed. "You really don't have much confidence in our judicial system, do you?"

"I'm sure there are comparable gaps in ours, but I must admit, I haven't been impressed." Finley crossed her arms and sat back in her chair. "Is Manzo available or not?"

"It appears he is in a meeting. But he should be out shortly," the man responded apologetically. "He is a busy man."

"I'm sure he is, but busy or not, time waits for no man." Finley stood up, and Max did the same. "You have our number. Call us and let us know when Grant will be released."

"Ms. Blake, you can't expect everything to work so quickly. The police will have to review the evidence and how the confession was secured. Officer Manzo will also want to talk to you about your abduction. There is a lot to be done. You must understand."

Finley leaned toward Assardi, her voice firm but calm, the Southern syrup almost dripping off every syllable.

"I understand. I do. I understand that unless the police move immediately on finding and arresting the confessor, my adduction and the lack of police response to it will become an international incident."

She continued, tapping the envelope on the attorney's desk as she spoke. "Since Officer Manzo doesn't have time to come see me, I will graciously go see him. We're heading over to the police station to report the kidnapping. You can deliver the confession later. When we get the same response to my situation as we have to Grant's, my next stop will be the American embassy. I'm sure there will be interest there."

Finley was down the stairs and across the square before Max could catch up. "What was that back there? Assardi has been our ally. Why did you put him on the hot seat like that?"

"Because he and Manzo are friends. I'm sure both are decent men, but they go along to get along." She stopped and turned to face Max. "They can put any number of spins on Grant's involvement in Blaine's death, but they can't twist my abduction into anything other than police incompetence. Neither Assardi nor Manzo wants that to happen."

She started back toward the police station with Max hurrying after her.

"So, in essence, you're threatening the ones you know have a conscience to get the rest of them to do their jobs."

"In essence."

Finley's report of her kidnapping by Marc and her rescue by "two kindly gentlemen who saw her in distress" was short and sweet. The desk officer took the statement and placed it on top of a stack of other official-looking documents before going back to looking at his newspaper.

"I suspect in the next hour, that report—and Officer Manzo—will be over in Assardi's office, and about an hour after that, we will get a call, summoning us for a cordial conversation." Finley laughed as she descended the stairs. "In the meantime, we need to find Marc. But I need another coffee before we figure out how to make that happen."

Max put his arm around Finley's shoulders and led her up to the café that had become their haunt. For the first round of espressos and pastries, both Max and Finley sat silently, enjoying their food. By the second round of coffee, Finley had come back to life, and she and Max were researching towns and villages on the way to the long ferry to Croatia.

"I think that is going to be his escape route. He isn't going to want to stay in Italy long, so driving to Croatia would be risky. He also is going to avoid the airport, which leaves out Corsica," Finley said.

"He could hire a boat for any of those options."

"True, but they all require a fairly long drive within the Italian border. No, I think he's going to cut across to Ancona and take a boat to either Zadar or Split."

"But first, he'll get the loot to fund his passage." Max offered Finley the last piece of his *fiocchi di neve*. When she declined, he quickly popped it in his mouth and smiled in satisfaction.

"Yep, and that is where I'm stumped. How do we find him after the jewelry recovery but before the ferry to Croatia?"

"I have a question for *you* that may answer that. I know Vittorio said the car Marc put you in wasn't the one he had before. But when did he switch? I suspect it was *after* he moved Blaine to the well."

"Which is likely after he took the jewelry." Finley could see where Max was going with this. "If they have the tracking info for his movements before he switched cars, maybe we can narrow the search area."

She leaned over and kissed him hard. "You are brilliant!"

"For a kiss like that, I will strive to be brilliant every day!" Max smiled before calling Vittorio. "Vittorio's number should still be in my phone."

While Max explained to Vittorio what they needed, Finley checked the ferry schedules. There appeared to be two ferry lines that worked the middle part of the Adriatic going to Split and Zadar, each running two schedules. There would be a ferry leaving today at 2:30 p.m. and another leaving tomorrow at 11:00 a.m. To get earlier or later departures, one had to go to Venice or Bari.

He might try for the 2:30 p.m. If he's smart, he'll get the jewelry as soon as he can. If so, he can just make the two-hour drive to catch the ferry today and be on his way to freedom.

"What'd he say?" Finley asked when Max got off the phone.

"He thinks they still have it and can pull it. They'll give us a call." Max looked over at the scribbles on Finley's pad. "What's that?"

"The ferry schedule. If Vittorio and Aldo can help narrow the search area for us, we may be able to get the police to set up a discreet corridor between here"—she traced the route for Max—"where he picks up the jewels, and Ancona, where he needs to catch the next ferry, which is at two thirty p.m."

"Good thinking." Max winked his appreciation. "I suspect the jewels aren't going to be far from where he dumped her body."

"You're probably right. I'll call Elena and let her know we may be trespassing on her property." Finley rummaged around in her bag until she found her phone.

She gently tapped Max's arm. "Can you call Assardi and ask him to alert his buddy Officer Manzo, so they can provide backup when Marc starts to run? Tell him about the ferries." Finley raised a cynical eyebrow. "It's Manzo's call as to whether he wants to set up the intercepts."

Max ordered a couple of *lungos* while they each made their calls. "When we finish our coffees, we should get a move on."

Only a half hour later, they turned onto the lane that cut through the Fuscati estate. Finley had reached Elena and alerted her to the situation. She wanted to be sure there were no trufflers out, along with the dogs and their handlers. She had no idea how Marc would react if cornered.

Vittorio and Aldo had called with the location pins for the last several times the transponder from Marc previous car had communicated. All were on or near the Fuscatis' property. Max's hunch had been right. Max and Vittorio hatched a plan, one that allowed for police involvement but didn't count on it.

With everyone in position, Max and Finley inched up the path, looking for movement. Not far from the well, they got out of the car and began walking up the trail.

"You see anything?" Max whispered.

Finley had just shaken her head when she spotted movement in the bushes on the edge of the clearing. The cropping in the adjacent forest was cleared of underbrush but offered nice dense cover at waist level along its edges. She and Max moved into the woods on the other side of the meadow and watched. From their angle, they could discern movement but without any clarity as to whether it was man or beast.

"Should we move closer?" Finley mouthed to Max.

He raised his hand to signal her to wait. After a short time, a man raised from his crouched position and walked away. Max motioned for Finley to stay put. In time, Marc, now fully visible, came back to the cropping with a shovel and a bag in hand. Finley drew a breath and held it. She and Max traded knowing glances.

I wonder if Aldo has him in view. She didn't dare risk pulling out her phone and having the sun's reflection or some other anomaly tip off Marc to their presence.

From their position, they could hear Marc cutting the earth with his shovel and setting it aside. He had a steady rhythm that he interrupted from time to time, presumably to wipe the sweat from his brow. Max and Finley took advantage of the digging cadence to reposition themselves. From their new vantage, they had clear line of sight to the hole being dug, but branches covered the digger's face. After a good twenty minutes of digging, the sounds stopped.

Marc crouched down again and reached for the sack. He dug deep into the hole and pulled out a dirty drawstring bag. Opening it, he rummaged around in it, taking out what looked like clothes, before shoving the clothes back inside and dropping the bag down the burrow again. He leaned far into the hole and drew out another earth-stained bag, which he weighed in his hand before peering inside. A satisfied smile crept across his face like the sunrise until he was grinning from ear to ear. He pushed what appeared to be other sacks that he had taken out back into their hiding place and started to fill in the hollow. Midmotion, he paused.

Max and Finley understood why. On the far side of the meadow, they could hear voices. Vittorio and Aldo throwing up a diversion? But that wasn't the plan. It sounded like a woman as the voices grew nearer. Elena had been warned. Finley realized the accent was different, not Italian. French, maybe? Whoever it was, Marc dropped to his stomach and waited.

"I think we can set up the easels here," the woman said as she neared the edge of the large meadow that occupied the other side of the lane. Her back was to them as her arm swept the panorama she proposed to paint.

Of all times! Pray that he gets in his car and drives away with his stash.

"We have a lot of space to play with so we can spread out," the woman continued as Finley heard the sounds of equipment dropping to the ground and metal sliding, presumably the easels engaging.

Get in your car, Marc. Get in the car. Drive away! Vittorio or the police—if they've decided to play along—can catch you at the gate. No need for a shoot-out.

But Marc had other plans. After a long period of waiting, he suddenly shot up from his hiding place, the bag clutched to his chest, and took off like a scared rabbit. Instead of running to his car, he struck off in the other direction, passing only a hair's breadth from Max and Finley's perch.

The sudden movement caught the attention of the painters, who stood in stunned suspense while Marc ran along a low dividing fence between the Fuscati estate and the adjoining property. In a single fluid motion, he vaulted over the fence and sprinted across the meadow.

Max had attempted to grab the man as he ran past but missed. Soon, both he and Finley were running after him full tilt.

Finley recognized the artists as Oktavia Martin, Gary, and Pierre, their dinner companions from a few days ago. "Call the police!" she shouted as she cleared the fence onto the other property. "It's Finley Blake. Call the police—now!"

While Max tried to close in on Marc, Finley swung wide, hoping to trap him between herself and Max as he closed in on the far fence. She had yet to see Aldo and figured he was in his car farther down the opposite lane, waiting for some action or further instruction. All of a sudden, Marc changed direction and started directly at Finley. She paused for a moment to gauge his proposed direction. For a minute, she and Marc squared off, defensively shifting direction like players on a football field.

From her peripheral vision, Finley could see other figures rushing toward her. *Gary and Pierre*, she imagined. Seeing no gun, she maintained her position, charging Marc at times to push him closer to Max, who was stationed behind him. Now, she heard the sound of dogs barking, the thunder of their paws hitting the ground. *Big dogs. Here comes the cavalry.*

"Marc, give it up. You're surrounded. If you get past us, there are police all over the woods and blocking the gates. Don't make them shoot you! Stop! Give yourself up!" she cried.

Before he had a chance to decide, one of the dogs, a Rottweiler, was on him, Marc's arm firmly in his jaws. Gary and Max reached Marc shortly thereafter, and Pierre called off the dogs.

Obediently, the one with Marc's arm dropped it from his mouth, and the other removed his massive paw from Marc's chest. They sat and waited for a further command. When none came, they lay down and surveyed their prey.

While Max and Gary pulled Marc to his feet, Finley ran to recover the sack that Marc had dropped in his attempt to get away. It was heavy. Finley opened the bag slightly and looked inside. Blaine's jewelry—and the gun. She pulled her phone from her pocket and dialed Vittorio. In seconds, sirens filled the air as at least five police cars descended from two angles.

"You okay?" Max called to her. She gave him a thumbs-up in reply.

When the police had taken Marc away, Finley and the others headed to where Oktavia was waiting. "Sacrebleu, what was all that? It looked like you were filming something for the cinema!"

Finley laughed as she saw Max retrieve her satchel and camera from the other field. "More like reality TV." She turned to Gary and Pierre, who were gathering the dogs. "And thanks to you two and your beautiful friends here. I didn't hear the dogs earlier, so I was as surprised as Marc to see them come running. Our heroes."

"Who was that man?" Pierre asked, sitting on a camp chair to recover his breath.

"Marc Santori, the man who killed the woman in the well. Accidentally, but he still killed her."

"What was he doing here?" Gary had moved to Pierre and touched his back gently to assess the older man's condition.

Max joined the group now and passed Finley her satchel. "He had buried some jewelry for safekeeping, and he came back to get it to make his getaway."

"I had alerted Elena that we thought he was coming here, but we hadn't expected you," Finley said.

"Goodness, we might have been killed—unwitting victims!" Oktavia gushed dramatically.

"Fortunately, he didn't have his gun this time," Max explained.

Finley cleared her throat and pulled the weapon from the bag with a frown. "Yes, he did."

Max and the others gasped.

"Gracious. The gods were with us yet again." Max exhaled and took Finley's arm as she dropped the gun back into the bag. "We'd better get that over to Officer Manzo."

Finley gave the dogs each a pat before throwing her hand up in farewell.

"Did you know about the gun?" Max asked quietly as they walked away.

Finley shook her head. "Nope. Saw it when I checked the sack. We were lucky. *Very* lucky."

Officer Manzo was waiting for them when they neared the police cars. Marc was cuffed in the back seat of one of the cars as the flood of officers wandered the woods and the field, picking up bits of evidence as they went.

"I think you'll find Blaine's clothes in the trough he dug. He didn't have time to fill it in, so it should be easy to spot," Finley said, pointing to the area where Marc had been digging.

"How did you know he would come here?" The officer scowled.

"What, are you going to accuse us of being in cahoots with Marc and Grant now?" Finley countered. "We found them by doing basic investigative work. Plain and simple."

Max touched Finley's arm gently before he spoke. "We weren't sure where you were in your investigation. We didn't mean to interfere, but we also didn't want him to get away."

Manzo laughed. "Basically, you did our work for us. *Scusi,* but we wanted to be careful. You have solved both the murder and the robbery in less time than it would have taken us to do the administrative paperwork. I assure you, we will move faster to release your friend. I promise."

Finley and Max acknowledged his informal apology and headed to where Vittorio and Aldo were standing. Vittorio was sartorial in a coffee-colored linen suit and his trademark white Panama.

"*Bon giorno!*" he greeted them cheerily. "Nice morning for an arrest, is it not?"

Aldo chuckled. "We got to sit in the cool air while you work. I saw it all. *Impressionante.*"

"Mafaldo said the signora has 'moves.' Smart, pretty, and as you say in your movies, badass?" Vittorio commented.

"That she is!" Max pulled Finley close and kissed her hair. "I think it's time for a proper breakfast—or is it lunch? In any event, I'm sure Sofia won't mind if you come back to the house and join us."

19

"**WE'RE BACK! AND WE HAVE** company," Max announced when he opened the door.

Sofia met him in the hall with a big kiss and a worried look. "Did you find him?"

Vittorio answered for Max, pushing open the door to give Sofia a hug and double kisses. Aldo greeted her as well.

"Come in, come in! Please head out to the terrace, and I will get food and drinks. I didn't know when you were coming so I only prepared cold foods, leftovers," Sofia apologized.

Chuck chortled as he welcomed them onto the terrace. "But there's a lot of it, so we'll still eat well!"

While Finley went to help Sofia in the kitchen, Max took care of serving the drinks.

Chuck was chomping at the bit for news of what happened. "You caught him, I take it? Was he where you thought he'd be?"

"Yes to both, but this is Finley's story to tell," Max told him. "You would have thought it was Super Bowl Sunday the way she covered him."

"Did that little lady tackle him?" Chuck pressed Max for more information.

"She looked ready to, but then reinforcements came," Max teased as Finley and Sofia came back into the room with platters of chicken, pasta, and pork.

"Let's move over to the table and eat while we talk." Sofia ushered her guests to the large wooden dining table, while Finley moved the cheeses, salamis, and bread from the sideboard to the table.

Aldo sighed as he sat down. "Heaven. I am in food heaven!"

"You keep this up, she'll be setting a place for you every Sunday," Chuck scoffed. "Fill your plates so you can tell us what happened."

Everyone did as they were told while Max pulled out another bottle of red for the table and poured Finley her glass of white.

"Who wants to start?" Max asked, looking among Finley, Vittorio, and Aldo.

Vittorio bowed graciously toward Finley. "This is her—your—story. Mafaldo and I were watching from the sides with only a part view."

"Fin?" Max deferred.

"Not much to tell. When we got to Elena's, Marc was already there, preparing to dig. We could see him, and then he started digging in earnest."

"We used that as our chance to move a little closer, so we could see what he was doing," Max added. "All the while, Finley had her lens on him."

"Yeah, he dug for quite a while, and then he started pulling stuff out of a hole. Some of it looked like clothes."

"That poor woman's clothes," Sofia cried softly.

Finley nodded. "Seems so. When he found the bag of jewelry, he started to fill in the hole, but then Oktavia, Pierre, and Gary came along for a day of landscape painting. I didn't know her field abuts Elena and Mario's place."

"Did they scupper the operation, then?" Chuck asked excitedly.

"No, Marc hid when he heard them, and we just waited," Max added.

"I was praying he would just casually throw up his hand in greeting, get in his car, and get out of there," Finley said. "But he made a run for it."

"Jumped over the fence. Startled poor Oktavia, who just froze."

"I was screaming for them to call the police while I took off after Marc and Max."

"Finley smartly didn't follow directly behind me but went wide to sort of trap him, but when he neared the fence, which was bigger on that side than the other, he decide to turn back and head toward Finley."

"Did he have his gun?" Chuck asked, his brow knitted.

"We didn't think so. He was just clutching this sack that we figured had the jewelry in it," Finley said.

"So, he turns on Finley, and my girl didn't back down. She matched him move for move. He jigged left; she jigged right. He jagged right; she caught him on the left. Some of the best coverage I've seen," Max relayed with a smile.

Finley laughed. "I just didn't want him to get away."

Max went on. "All of a sudden, he pivots and darts away down the field with me, Finley, and now Gary and Pierre on his tail. And then, out of nowhere come these dogs, which tackled him downfield and sat on him until Pierre called them off."

"It really was like scene from movie!" Vittorio recounted. "When I see the man jump over fence, I call police. They were on ready. Said little lady say to be ready or else. So, they ready!"

Finley chuckled. *I guess going all Mama on Assardi worked. Thank goodness.*

"They came and cuffed Marc and took him away," Max concluded, wrapping up the story.

"Marc had dropped the sack when he did the last pivot. Must have lost his footing and decided getting away was more important," Finley said. "In any event, I picked it up while Max and the other guys were securing Marc."

"Were the jewels inside?" Chuck asked.

"The jewels—and the gun. We were lucky. It could have been bad. Really bad."

The table quieted for a moment as the impact of Finley's statement sunk in.

"Well, it all ended well." Chuck raised his glass. "To a successful conclusion to this really convoluted case!"

When the toasts were finished, Sofia asked, "When will Grant be released?"

"I hope soon. Very soon, so he can go home and fight for his children," Finley said.

"Have you told Evans yet?" Max inquired of Vittorio as they sat on the terrace after lunch.

"Yes, I phoned him as I come here. He was occupied, of course, but glad it is over."

"Well, thanks. We'll call him later this evening to express our gratitude," Finley said. "He knew just what we needed. You two! We can't thank you enough."

Vittorio and Aldo stood to leave. "The pleasure was totally ours," Vittorio said. He turned to Max. "This one is 'hard to hold but worth the effort,' as my mama says. *Ne vale assolutamente la pena.*"

The two couples had just settled back on the terrace, refilled glasses of wine in hand, when there was a knock on the door. Sofia got up to answer it.

When she returned, Assardi and Manzo were with her.

"So sorry for interrupting your afternoon," the officer said. "We wanted to let you know the latest in the Lambert case."

"Well, before you start, can we offer you a glass of wine or coffee?" Sofia, forever the perfect hostess, asked.

The attorney looked at Manzo, shrugged, and said, "A small glass of wine, maybe. It's close to the end of the day."

They laughed lightly while Max grabbed the bottle and some glasses and began to pour.

"Did Marc confirm the confession?" Finley asked, taking a sip of her wine.

Officer Manzo nodded. "He did confirm it. He said he didn't try to hurt her. She came at him like a *strega*, and he pushed her away. Mr. Lambert had said the same thing about the bruises on the woman. Hard to believe, but we confirmed with his doctor."

"You could have done that earlier! We told you all of this, and you let him sit in jail all that time." Finley's face flushed red.

"I know. We are very sorry. We were trying to be careful. We don't get a lot of murder in this area, so we moved cautiously," Manzo explained.

"But in the meantime, the man runs the risk of having his children taken from him, his reputation ruined, his future destroyed. All for something he didn't do—couldn't have done." Finley was beyond angry now. The thought of Grant's children being told lies about him was deplorable.

"We are moving to talk to the judge tomorrow morning so that soon, very soon, he can go home," Assardi said. "I must apologize, too, for not being as vigorous an advocate for Grant as I should have been. We are used to things moving slowly here, and we get suspicious when they move too fast."

"Mr. Santori told us, too, where he put her clothes and how he moved the body. He explained all," Manzo added.

"How did he get her out of there? There was a very narrow window between the time I almost ran into him and when we found her body," Finley wondered.

"He remembered seeing you and knew you had taken a picture of his car. So he went around and entered the village through the fields, wrapped her up, and took her to the well. He remembered the old well from when he was a boy and used to play in the woods with his cousins." Manzo took a sip of his wine and smiled appreciatively.

Finley sighed. "But before he threw her down the well, he took all her jewelry off and buried it with her other clothes."

"He said it took him a while because he had to bury it deep. He didn't want the dogs to pick up the scent," the officer continued.

"Did he say where he hoped to go if he had gotten away?" Max asked.

"To Zadar. He was going to take the ferry. He thought Split had too many foreigners. People who might have seen his face in the newspapers. He was going to head inland to a village," Assardi said.

"Are you going to represent him?" Finley was curious. She wasn't sure she would want him as her defense attorney if she were Marc. He knew too much.

The attorney shook his head. "No, it is better that someone else defend him. Not I."

After some general conversation about the weather and truffling this season, the two took their leave. The foursome was quiet for several minutes after they left. It had been an eventful morning, and Sofia announced it was going to be a packed evening as well.

"Finley told me in the kitchen that you are going to be leaving us tomorrow, so I invited a few of the people who greeted you for an impromptu farewell tonight. Just pastas and salads. And friendship."

Max looked surprised, but Finley simply smiled as they all trundled off to their afternoon naps.

Upstairs, Max observed Finley as she started to pack her things in her duffel in preparation for their departure tomorrow.

"Is there an assignment you need to get back to tomorrow?" he asked as he watched her slim figure move about the room.

"No, nothing in particular. I know you probably wanted to spend a bit more time with Chuck and Sofia, and I'm sorry."

"But . . . ?" Max intoned.

She crawled across her side of the bed until she reached him. "But I wanted to surprise you."

"Surprise me? With what?"

"With a little something special. If I tell you, it won't be a surprise." She leaned in and kissed him long and hard. "And I wanted you to myself. Selfish, I know, especially under the circumstances. But I couldn't help myself."

"Well, you are never selfish, so this must have been a compelling need," Max suggested, kissing her nose.

"It was, I assure you. They'll drop a car off for us tomorrow morning, and we can head out any time after that. So, we can laze about with Sofia and Chuck until we decide to go. I'll drive, of course."

"When did you have time to plan all of this?" Max ruffled her hair. "You've barely had time to go to the bathroom, and you still managed to concoct this elaborate plan. I'm impressed."

"I have my ways," Finley crooned slyly. "Now, I need a nap if we're going to party all night!"

Finley and Max walked into a room that was buzzing with energy. Chuck was playing a mix of blues standards from Buddy Guy, Eric Clapton, and Stevie Ray Vaughan as their friends grabbed wine and sat on the benches, chairs, and cushions that were scattered around the terrace. When they entered, Chuck stopped his playing and started clapping.

"The guests of honor. Our own Holmes and Watson!" He laughed as others joined in the applause. "I'm not going to get into who's Holmes and who's Watson. Don't want to wreck a marriage!"

The guests laughed and greeted Finley and Max. Sofia brought Finley a prosecco and Max a Sangiovese. "Unless you would prefer something else?"

Finley answered her with a kiss on the cheek. "This is perfect! As has been everything about our stay. We are going to miss you terribly."

Max agreed. "You have an open invitation to visit us in London, but I know traveling with ALS is hard."

"Yes, but you never know. If it holds for a while like it is now, we can get around pretty well in the air and on the ground. It is just if it decides to move upward." Sofia gave a sad shrug.

"Well, if it moves, then we'll come to you, assuming we haven't worn out our welcome. My mama always says fish and houseguests start to stink after three days. And we have been here far longer than that," Finley said.

"Never! I haven't seen him this happy in a long time. Do come back. Soon!" Sofia begged.

Finley and Max made their way onto the terrace, which seemed more crowded than it had when they first arrived. Finley looked around. The same couples were there—Gary and Pierre, Oktavia and Laurent, Amata and Silvano, Elena and Mario, but she also saw Vittorio and a few others she didn't know. She wondered where Aldo had gone.

"Vittorio, so good to see you here." Finley pressed kisses to both of his cheeks. "Where is Aldo, though?"

"Already on another assignment. A very busy man." Vittorio smiled elegantly. "Sofia was so gracious to include me in your farewell. I think you stay longer, but no, you go tomorrow."

"We'll be back, now that Max and Chuck have found each other again. And London to Rome is a short flight." She started getting a bit teary at the thought of leaving Sofia and Chuck, given the precarious nature of Chuck's disease. She mentally promised that she would talk to Sofia about a good time for their next visit, before either she or Max were called back on the road.

"Congratulations on apprehending that woman's killer, though it sounds tragic all around," Elena said as she and Oktavia descended upon Finley after Vittorio moved on to talk to Gary and Amata. "Oktavia said the chase was very exciting. Are you and Max in the police? I thought you were a photographer."

Finley laughed. "Max and I are hardly police officers. We just get caught in interesting situations sometimes. And yes, I am a photographer and travel writer. Sometimes the photography comes in handy in solving whatever crimes we happen to get involved in."

"So, this isn't your first murder?" Oktavia gave Elena a wary side-glance while she waited for Finley's response.

Finley was careful with her words. "We don't seek them out, but there have been others that have found their way to us."

Oktavia threw her head back and gave a hearty laugh. "You are delightful. How many murders have you been involved with? And always with your deliciously handsome husband, or do you engage others in these endeavors?"

"I haven't stopped to count, but there have been several. Mainly it's my sister and I who get in pickles, but Max; my sister's husband, David; and Evans, a friend of ours who is at Interpol, often help. My mama and daddy have just given up. As long as we make it out in one piece, I guess it's fine."

"Goodness me! I was joking when I asked, but you really are serious when you say you and your sister get into a lot of scrapes." Oktavia took a long gulp of her wine.

"Vittorio and Max say it was an accident, the woman's death. Do you believe that, or is he getting away with murder?" Elena asked.

Finley thought of the anguish in both Grant's and Marc's voices when they spoke of Blaine's vicious tantrums and their vain attempts to keep her at bay. "I really do believe it was an accident. An unfortunate accident."

"What happens now?" Elena asked.

"I guess Marc will be tried for manslaughter and robbery, and Grant will be released to go home to his family. Maybe he will be able to put his life back together. I hope so, for the children's sake," Finley said.

"I'm curious. What was it that was different about this case from some of the others you've been involved with?" Elena wondered.

Finley set her glass down on the side table and leaned back. "I think that it was so personal. For all involved—Grant, Marc, Blaine, and then me. Once I was in it, there was no stepping away."

"So, what's next? Some other exotic place? Sofia was listing some of the places you have been—Jaipur, Palawan, Galle. Where are you off to now?" Oktavia leaned forward to get the answer.

"It's a surprise, but I'm kidnapping Max to spend a few days in Argentario. I considered Portofino, but I didn't really want to spend our whole time driving," Finley whispered to the clustered women.

"Are you staying at Il Pellicano?" Elena asked and then sighed deeply when Finley nodded. "I have never been, but it is on my basket list. Is that what you call it?"

"Bucket list. And yes, I've heard it is pretty special. So, it'll be a nice post-case treat!"

The hotel, once a romantic hideaway in Argentario for an American socialite and her dashing British aviator, was purported to be a sparkling gem on the Mediterranean Sea set into the cliff above the ocean. Finley was glad that Blaine's killer had been caught, and she and Max could find time to sneak away.

20

MAX AND FINLEY LAZED IN bed the next morning, the shutters thrown open to the new day, the olive hills tinged with a salmon glaze as the sun came up over their crest. They dressed slowly, savoring the last moments of what had been an extraordinary trip, not just because of the challenges in resolving Grant's dilemma but also because of the pleasure in getting to know Sofia and Chuck better and enjoying their Mediterranean lifestyle.

"Remember I told you a few days ago that I wasn't ready to slip into this pace of life just yet?" Finley said while slipping on a persimmon-colored linen wrap dress with a deep V neckline and patch pockets.

"Yeah." Max finished tucking his navy cotton shirt into his jeans and smiled. "You changed your mind? You're going make me seasick with all the shifting from side to side."

"Don't be silly. I haven't been that wishy-washy," Finley countered. "I think it was the notion of doing this all the time, like, every day, that I resisted. But I could easily do this for a couple of months out of the year. Eating, drinking, talking on the terrace."

"I will keep that in mind. Another thing about you to tuck away."

"And blackmail me with when I'm rushing about, harried, on our next holiday?" Finley teased. She was known for taking a week or more to decompress fully on vacations. She hoped the next few days would be an exception.

"No, but that is a thought!" Max put the last of his things in his leather carry-on and sat at the foot of the bed, watching her. "No, something to consider when we talk about where to go next, what to do, how fast to pace things."

He got up and pulled her close. "You know I want kids. And I know you want them too, but maybe not just yet. So, while we're thinking about kids and where to live and how to live, these things are important for me to understand and factor into the equation."

Finley turned in his arms to face him. "A lot of things to think about and a whole lifetime to figure them out." She kissed his nose. "Sorry to break the moment, but right now, all I want to think about is coffee. Last night was fun, but it went on for a long time after I was ready for bed."

"Agreed, but I don't know that I would've really wanted it to end sooner. It may be the last time Chuck can play an all-night gig. I didn't let him know, but Sofia and I were recording the whole thing."

"As she said—for her. What a lovely gift to be able to listen to him when he can't play anymore."

Max nodded and opened the door for them to go downstairs to breakfast.

Sofia was just heading into the kitchen when they reached the main hall. She turned briefly before darting behind the door. She called out as it closed, "Let Chuck keep you company while I finish up with breakfast."

While Max walked out onto the terrace, Finley stuck her head into the kitchen to see if she could help and was quickly shooed out. Chastened, she joined Max outside.

"Grab yourself a cup of Joe and take a seat. She's been bustling about in there like she's cooking for the Light Brigade!" Chuck laughed. "I just do what I always do—make myself scarce."

Finley leaned over and kissed Chuck's forehead as she headed to the sideboard for coffee. "You ready for a top-up? What time did you turn in? You don't seem any worse for wear."

"No to the coffee. Sofia just poured me a fresh cup." Chuck lifted his cup to show her it was full to the brim. "We turned in not long after you did. Around two or so. The moon was out, so Sofia and I just sat here looking at the stars for a bit. A glorious night."

"It was," Finley concurred as she poured herself and Max cups of coffee. "And despite all the drama with Grant, this has been a memorable time with you and Sofia. I'm so glad I finally got to meet you."

"Come here, girl, and let me give you a hug," Chuck said, reaching out his arms. "I never thought this boy would settle down. Not that there wasn't a line of women who would've sawed off their right leg to be with him.

"All I'm saying," he continued, his arm around Finley's waist, "is that when he said he'd found you again, I hoped you'd be the one."

"Well, I was and am and always will be the one and only for him, and he for me." Finley kissed Chuck again before taking her seat on the bench beside him that looked over the hills. The morning mist was burning off, and the gold of the dusty fields reflected brightly in sun.

"Lucky man," Chuck murmured.

"Yep, very lucky man," Max said, gazing lovingly at Finley.

They sat like that in peaceful silence for several minutes, until Sofia returned with a large spinach frittata and fat fried sausages.

"I kept promising you sausages, and you never had time to eat them in the morning. Some I used for the polenta earlier in the week, but last night, Elena brought over some that have truffle shavings in them, and I knew just what I wanted to fix for breakfast this morning. Come, let's eat."

The morning passed slowly, like a long cat stretch that released all the tension of the week and settled calm in their bones. Sometime during the morning, Finley had sent Vittorio a shot of him perfectly framed against the Spoleto church arches, a study in contrasts that she was beginning to prize. She chuckled at his response.

"Bella, thank you for putting me in your lovely composition. *Scusi*, my suit is a little wrinkled!"

They were still around the table when they heard a tap at the door. "Who could that be?" Sofia asked as she rose to answer it.

"Could be that lawyer fellow or maybe the officer saying they lost the confession and are still holding Grant," Chuck kidded.

It was neither. Grant himself entered quietly, almost shyly.

Finley and Max jumped up to greet him as Sofia guided him into the room and offered him breakfast.

"No, thank you. I can't stay long. I'm on my way to the airport. The judge cleared me last night and let me book a flight for today. Nice country and all, but I think I need to head home," he said. "I just came to get my bags."

"Of course." Finley touched his elbow and drew him farther into the room. "Are you sure you can't stop for even a coffee?"

Grant demurred, standing in the middle of the room, his hands clasped as if he held a hat. He looked awkward as he searched for the right words. "I also wanted to thank all of you for your support through this ordeal. I don't know that I would have survived it without your efforts."

"We only did what was necessary," Finley stated as Max brought the two duffel bags and backpack downstairs.

"You know that's not true. Even if you weren't doing it for me but for the girls, the result is still the same." Grant gave an apprecia-tive smile. "I secured an attorney to help me fight Blaine's parents for custody. Once that happens, I'll get the firm to transfer me to Singapore or Bangkok, someplace far away from this nightmare."

Max set the bags down and extended his hand. "Glad we could help. All the best getting your kids back."

Grant shook it and said softly, "I knew she was sick. I didn't get her the help she needed early enough. I was too concerned about appearances. I thought it would just go away. But it didn't."

The group listened solemnly to what Grant said. Finley knew how hard any admission of weakness or error was for Grant. He continued, "That'll change. I plan to raise the girls differently now. Maybe if I had listened to Finley all those years ago, none of this would have happened."

He walked over to shake Chuck's hand and give Sofia kisses on both cheeks before turning to Finley and Max. "Finley, I can't thank you enough. I prayed, but I never would have imagined in a million years how you fought for me."

Finley reached up and kissed his cheek. She stepped back and joked, "I told you a long time ago, you're family. Once you're marked as ours, Mama never lets you go."

Grant chuckled before addressing Max. "Max, I've got to give it to you, man, for being a real stand-up guy. Fighting for me right alongside her. Not many husbands would have done that. But then, she is some kind of woman. Look after her."

Max shook his hand again. "That she is. That she is."

After helping Grant load his bags into the waiting taxi, Max returned inside. Finley, Sofia, and Chuck had left the table and taken chairs on the terrace. Max grabbed his coffee cup from the table and joined them.

"What did he mean about listening to what you said?" Max asked Finley as he claimed a seat beside her.

Finley laughed softly and sighed. "I think I had already decided to leave, but I kept trying to get through to him. He had a set idea of what life was supposed to look like. That was what he defined as success. It was all a facade. It didn't matter if you were happy or not."

She continued, "I told him that when what others think matters more to you than the ones you're close to, it's time to hang it up."

"Harsh, but true," Chuck muttered. "So true."

"Look, we had better head on down the road before it gets too late." Max took the last gulp of his coffee and stood to leave. "Finley knows where she is going, but I haven't the slightest idea, so if she gets lost, I can't help her."

"I know where I'm going. I think. And if we get lost, we'll still have a nice adventure!" Finley kissed his cheek and headed upstairs to make last-minute preparations.

The goodbyes were bittersweet, but Finley promised Sofia they would find time in the next month for a quick trip to get a refill on good friends, good food, and good times.

Max and Finley traveled in silence until they reached Acquasparta, a good twenty minutes from the house.

Finley spoke first, taking a side-glance at her husband. "Thank you for introducing me to those two. Wish you had shared them earlier, but glad you shared them now."

"I wasn't keeping them from you. We just drifted apart, each doing our own version of life," Max declared. "Sorry Grant got in a bind, but I'm glad he provided me with the opportunity to reconnect with Chuck."

"Yeah," Finley mused. "I hope Grant gets his girls back. I agree that getting far away will help all of them recover."

Max murmured his assent and then changed the subject. "So, where are we going again?"

"You can't trick me into telling you. This is a secret."

Conceding defeat, Max pushed back his seat, rolled down his window, and enjoyed the cheesy Eurovision mix playing on the Italian radio for the next two plus hours. When they pulled onto the narrow strip of land that led to a little fishing village, Max didn't care where he was going. He loved where he was.

"What is this place?" He looked around at the terra-cotta buildings, the striped umbrellas over the charming café tables, the large, open cobbled stone square where children on bikes traded places with the cars that inched across the plaza to the restaurants and parking lot on the other side. On the pier just below the square, fishermen were packing up from the morning sales, ready for their own lunches before heading back out to sea later in the afternoon for the dinner catch. Regardless of the meal, fresh fish was assured.

"This is Porto Santo Stefano. I figured we would try to grab a late lunch or snack here before we headed to the hotel. Once we're there, I've been told we may not want to leave, and I wanted to see this little village." Finely slid into a parking space close to the water and got out of the car.

"How did you find out about this place?" Max grabbed her satchel from the back seat and passed it to her.

"One of the photographers was developing some pictures at the magazine a few years ago when I lived in New York, and they were from here. I fell in love with it and decided if I was ever close enough to visit, I would. So here we are."

"Are we staying near here?" Max surveyed the square, looking for a hotel that might be the place.

"Not far." Finley grinned at Max's determination to find out their ultimate destination but remained mum as she headed across the cobbled expanse to one of the restaurants that appeared to still be open.

"Are you still serving?" she asked in halting Italian. When she was met by a nod, she chose a seat that looked out onto the water.

"Since when do you speak Italian?" Max claimed the chair next to her and stared at her in amazement.

"Since my first trip to Rome when I was in college. It is extremely limited and rusty as heck because I never get to use it. But if it entails asking about food, I can get by."

"So why were you asking me to do all the talking this trip?" Max munched on a breadstick as he read over the menu.

"Because the conversation rarely revolved around food," Finley said. "It required more vocabulary and, quite honestly, more energy than I had."

Max took her hand and gently placed his lips on the inside of her wrist, his favorite spot. "I'm sorry you had to go through that. It must have been emotionally draining. As you said, divorced or not, he was—is—still family."

"No matter. It's over now." Finley leaned over and kissed him, taking her hand back in the same move. "What are you having?"

"I think fish of some kind, since we know it came in this morning. What about you?"

"Black ink pasta, my favorite."

"Really? I didn't think you were that fond of pasta, let alone with squid ink! Who knew?"

For the next hour or so, the two of them watched the sun crawl across the sky, no more in a hurry than they were. They ate, sipped their wine, read bits from the guidebook Finley had picked up while in Spoleto, and enjoyed the sun and the ease of life.

"Is there anything to see here?" Max asked, turning his chair and stretching his long body out to catch the sun.

"Not much. There is a fort, an aquarium, and the harbor, and that's about it. I'd like to take a few shots, but after that, we can head to Porto Ercole."

Max's ears perked up. "Is that where we're staying?"

Finley smiled at his almost childlike resolve to figure out the puzzle of where they were staying. As annoying as it could be at times, she knew that singular focus was what had gotten him through his painful childhood and drove his professional success.

Rising from her seat, she pecked his forehead. "Yes, dearest, that is where we'll be for the next couple of days. You said we needed to go on a proper honeymoon, so I decided to surprise you with a prelude. Short but hopefully sweet. I hope you like it."

"Any place with you, I know I'll love!"

The short drive from Porto Santo Stefano to the Il Pellicano was like a scene out of a movie. Boats bobbing in the crystalline harbor under an aquamarine sky on one side and curving, craggy hills dotted with long-needle scrub pine on the other. Finley had a flashback to driving in Carmel—the colors, the smells, the cliffs. The route passed through the town of Porto Ercole before continuing for several scenic kilometers. Finley came close to missing the discreet sign that directed her off the primary road and along the crest to the hotel.

They had almost reached the entrance to Il Pellicano when Max asked her the question. "We know Marc loved Grant, but did Grant love him?"

Finley needed time to respond.

They checked in, surveyed their room, and decided on a swim and sunbathing. Walking down the stone stairs that led from the main level of the boutique hotel to the pool that overlooked the azure sea, Finley continued to ponder Grant's possible feelings. When she had laid out her towel and settled in on the near empty deck, she replied.

"I think the whole relationship between the three of them was complicated. Grant loved his wife, but she couldn't love him like he needed her to. He found acceptance, comfort, and peace maybe with Marc, but it wasn't socially acceptable, as far as he was concerned. Marc just loved Grant and would have done—did—anything for him. And that's where it all fell apart."

"Sad. Really sad . . ." Max's voice tapered off, leaving the thought unfinished.

"Max, what is it you really wanted to ask?" Finley took his hand and held it while he searched for the words.

He paused and swallowed hard. "What I really wanted to ask . . ." He paused again.

"Yes?"

"What I wanted to know was whether Grant was capable of truly loving you."

Finley kissed his hand. She took her time again before she spoke. "Yes, I think so. But why do you ask?"

He turned and locked his eyes onto hers, giving her a rueful smile. "I've never said this out loud, but Fin, I've loved you from the first moment I saw you all those years ago in New York. But you were married. So I asked for the transfer to Morocco. It hurt too much to be near you."

Finley gasped quietly at the revelation and how different their story might have been had she known. She waited for him to go on.

"But you were hurting too. Sweetheart, had I known how controlling Grant was and how unhappy you were, I never would have left. I would've stayed to protect you, to comfort you. I'm sorry I left you to suffer."

"Max, it was nowhere near that dire. I was unhappy, yes, but I suspect your being there and me knowing how you felt only would have complicated matters." She brushed away a tear before he saw it. "It all worked out, and we're together now. So let's put it behind us and enjoy our little mini-moon."

Finley signaled the waiter to bring the bucket of Pol Roger Sir Winston Churchill they had been chilling for her. She poured two glasses and winked at Max. "In case you hadn't noticed, I love you to the moon and back."

He moved over to her lounge chair and took the glasses from her, setting them on the small table between them. Slowly, he took her in his arms. "And in case you hadn't noticed, I love you *more*." The last word was muffled by a deep, longing kiss.

The End

If you enjoyed this book and want to learn
more about Finley and Whitt Blake,
join our mailing list at www.mcarterfielding.com or
drop me a line at carter.fielding6554@gmail.com.
I'd love to hear from you.
Talk soon!

ABOUT THE AUTHOR

Carter Fielding is a millennial with an old soul. She likes old maps, old photographs, vintage records, and vintage champagnes. A Southerner with roots in Anderson, South Carolina, she likes a good bourbon, a day that calls for wearing a barn jacket and a pair of wellies, and the smell of wet earth after a good rain. She started writing the Blake Sisters series during lockdown to tame a wanderlust that couldn't be satisfied by a trip to Harris Teeter and ended up building a relationship with the whole cast of characters that has taken on a life of its own.

She lives in Northern Virginia with her Boykin Spaniel, Trucker, and uses her passion for books and travel to create characters she hopes readers will come to love.

ACKNOWLEDGMENTS

Another one done and dusted, but not without the help of legions of friends, family, and editors. As always, there is the production and distribution teams from Bublish, who put the finishing touches on my manuscript and get it ready for readers' hands.

And then there are the friends and family who seem to forever be in awe of the fact that a single kernel of a murderous idea can be massaged through two hundred plus pages of puzzles and twists and rabbit holes to reach a satisfying conclusion.

Finally, there are the readers—the beta readers who guide me during the drafting stages and the growing group of Fieldlings who keep me writing by sending notes asking when the next book is coming out.

New to the process are the members of my writers' critique group—Jutta and Lisa—who have seen parts of this book in its rawest of stages and have helped me redirect the storyline and polish the prose to another level of readability.

To all of you, my sincerest of thanks for your patience and commitment to helping me tell Finley and Whitt's stories. Until the next time . . .

9 781647 048778